The Diary

Of Jane

The Diary of Jane: Memoirs of Insanity

Kasey Thompson

Dark Moon Rising Publications | Virginia

Dark Moon Rising Publications

70 Foxwood Drive
Rocky Mount, Virginia   24151
Tel: (540) 257-2861

Any and all characters are a work of fiction.

ISBN-13: 978-1-945987-85-4

10 9 8 7 6 5 4 3 2 1

Printed in the United States of America

To the little girl who grows wildflowers in her soul

To you beautiful souls who have survived suicide attempts, who think it is the only answer, to those of you who harm yourselves, always know: You are beautiful just the way you are. Never give up! There are people out there who love you, care about you, and would give anything for you to see another day. The sun is rising. Just look to the horizon!

United States Numbers

National Suicide Prevention Hotline: 1-800-273-8255

Crisis Text Line: 741741

Someone is always waiting to help save your life and listen to you. Don't ever be afraid to speak to someone when you feel like all hope is lost <3

Other Works by Kasey Thompson

Tattered Pages Series: Surviving Sarah

Splintered

Future Releases

Tattered Pages Series: Remembering Sarah

Tattered Pages Series: Letting Sarah Go

Your demons don't love you. They're narcissists living rent-free in your head, telling you they do.

The Diary

Of Jane

Dear Diary,

People aren't born broken. People are made broken by society, by family, by people they love and care about. People are made broken by the mirror they see in other people's faces that morphs their own realities of what they see when they look in the actual mirror. It can happen at any moment in one's life. It can happen as a baby, as a toddler, as a child, as a teenager, or even as an adult. It can be the cold shoulder of a mother who doesn't hug their children or show affection. It can be the laughter of other children when they view you as different, funny-looking or fat. It can be the face of a teenage boy who had never been taught to respect others and instead spends every waking moment taking a dig at others to seem cooler. It can be the grown adult shouting out the window "whale" as they drive by you standing at a gas station. But as I said, people aren't born broken. They're molded into it, and I was not the exception.

I was born and named Christine Jane Addison, but everyone calls me Jane. I grew up in a poor county.

We didn't have a movie theater until I was in high school. It was the late 90s when we got our first Walmart. We had a Hardees, a Pizza Hut, a McDonald's, a Burger King, and a couple of Chinese restaurants. But that was it. There was nothing for teens to do except hang out in the Roses' parking lot at night. Where we lived was a dull place. Nothing extraordinary happened there, and even if we did have anything exciting to do there, I wouldn't have been allowed to experience it.

I was in my twenties when I realized I had never experienced true happiness. People often confuse happiness with laughter and having fun when people can laugh and have fun while still dreaming about slitting their wrists at night. A lonely, despairing feeling had overcome me, one that I couldn't shake. I had been on and off prescription depression pills since I was around twenty-four years old. I took them until I started feeling my mood change and then stopped. This process always gave me at least a year before the dark shroud dripped over my psyche and started putting the black thoughts back in my head. But that real expression of happiness, the one that makes you feel lighter than air without having to take prescription drugs or recreational drugs to achieve, I never felt that.

Don't get me wrong, the euphoric feeling from smoking weed was a nice feeling, but even that didn't equate to happiness. I had learned from an early age to just paint a smile on my face for everyone to see.

No one could fathom or understand why I was depressed, myself included. I once spoke to a guidance counselor after writing a suicide letter, and a friend turned the letter in, and she asked me that very question. Why are you depressed? I couldn't give her a reason why.... I didn't fucking know. I didn't understand how my brain was working at the time, and half the time still don't understand it. If I knew then what I know now, I could have easily told her because I don't know true happiness. I have never experienced the euphoria of childhood because I was never allowed to be a child. But my answer to her was that of a teenager. My parents are always yelling at me. People don't like me in school. I was socially inept.

She called my mother, and when I got home, instead of a loving, nurturing person wanting to sit down and talk to me about why I was unhappy, why I was depressed, why I had planned to kill myself... she yelled at me. She asked me if I wanted to be taken away because that is what would happen if I tried it. Not taken away to a mental institution, taken away as in put in foster care. The bare fact of the situation is she was more worried about getting in trouble as a parent rather than diagnosing her daughter's ailments. So, I never told anyone ever again that I was unhappy. I never told anyone again that I was depressed. And I never told anyone ever again that I had fantasies about slitting my wrists, or taking a whole bottle of pills, or even blowing my brains out.

People claim loneliness as an escape, as a reason to be around other people, to be in relationships, or to even ruin those relationships. The truth is, they don't truly comprehend the feeling of being lonely or feeling alone. It has nothing to do with someone being around you. You can be surrounded by a sea of people, a sea of people that sit and tell jokes with you, share intimacy with you, and call yourselves close friends, but those people mean nothing when that utter feeling of being completely alone hits you. It's in those dark moments that you are the most dangerous person in the room to yourself, and if you have no purpose, no reason to live, no day-to-day push or necessity to live to the next day, that you take the straight blade razor and end it. It's a black hole, sinking in quicksand feeling. And the more you struggle against the thoughts, the harder they suck you in until you are numb and unresponsive to those around you. A shell of the person you used to be. Before you say there are ways to make yourself self-love, save the bullshit. There is no amount of drugs, no amount of medications, no ease of this feeling. Read a depression bottle. The "cure," and I use cure very extremely lightly because it's not truly cured but merely staved off, for depression and suicidal thoughts have a side effect of depression and suicidal thoughts (meaning an increase in what you are already feeling.) If the pills didn't balance you right, they set what little balance you had off, and everything was worse. Have a slight emotional state? You suddenly start crying for no fucking reason. Get irritable a lot? Well, you have become the fucking Hulk of anger over an egg dropping on the floor and cracking.

I was twenty when I realized that alongside depression, I had a crippling anxiety issue. I had seen what abuse of anxiety medications did to people, so I tried to avoid the medications for as long as I could until I ended up on the floor with a crushing anxiety attack. I couldn't breathe, and the experience felt like a sugar drop. Afterward was then that I tried my hand at anxiety medicine to help me through along with my depression medication. By this time, I was prescribed Wellbutrin, Paxil, and Xanax. It was a nice little cocktail but wasn't nearly close to what I truly needed. The medications helped some, but the Xanax didn't keep the attacks at bay but helped during episodes when I needed fast relief. They switched me from Xanax to Klonopin, which had the opposite effects. Klonopin was good at keeping the attacks at bay, but when they hit, they were not fast-acting relief pills. I went on and off my medication for a while because the fact was, I truly couldn't afford them, and I no longer had insurance.

It was in my mid-twenties that the doctor who had been treating my depression and anxiety then diagnosed me alongside the two of them as bipolar. The doctor did what she wasn't supposed to do. She treated me for bipolar without evaluation. When you take bipolar medicine, they must create a perfect cocktail of medications for your depression so the medicines don't reverse one another. After about two months of taking the medicine, I was worse off than what I had been prior to the introduction of the bipolar medicine. I felt a shift in my psyche. So, I did what I thought was best. I stopped taking all the medication and just wrote out my pain. It took a couple of years for everything to catch up with me. That was when my sanity took a shift for the worse. I no longer felt sane. I felt like I was constantly drowning. When the loneliness started creeping into my bones and settled, those were the moments I floundered.

I had no one to turn to that I felt understood what I was going through. Everyone can say yes, I am bipolar, yes, I am depressed, yes, I have anxiety, but it's different case by case. No one KNEW how I FELT. And those I tried to tell would flip those feelings around on me. Why do you think you're depressed? What do you have to be depressed about? I DON'T FUCKING KNOW! I can't help my brain is making me feel this way. And then there were those who used my depression against me, saying that my mental health issues were causing them to lose their sanity. I didn't speak to them about my depression deeply. They just knew I was depressed and couldn't offer me the solace I needed, the boost to get my life back on track. These were the same people that I told I was walking on eggshells with anxiety, that I often felt utterly alone, and during the lonely state of mind I was in, I often imagined just ending it. There wasn't any compassion truthfully with their response of "You always know I am here for you." You may be there for me, but you can't understand why I am feeling this way because you aren't going through what I am. I felt like my friends were dropping off left and right because they were growing tired of the efforts of "helping" me or trying to "save" me.

Just like an addict can't get clean without deciding for themselves it's time (meaning you can't force them into sobriety), you can't force someone into being helped or saved from their depression. They are both chemical imbalances in the brain, one chemically induced from outside influences and one chemically induced from a malfunctioning brain. Trust me when I say I wanted to be saved. I wanted them to drag me from the pits of hell my own mind had created. But chemical imbalances aren't that simple, and depression has nothing to do with the will or not wanting to get better. Honestly, who the fuck wants to stay depressed and suicidal. My brain won't allow me to be saved. So, I spiral down a bottomless pit without any indication of when the end will come.

There are times when I try to explain to people what is going on that I tell them it's like demons are running amok in my head. They burn shit to the ground. They wreck friendships by not letting me process situations before I act on them. They throw baseballs at my glass house just to watch me glue the pieces back together so that they can shatter the walls over and over and laugh as I scramble to piece them back together. Whenever I am in a good mood, they always find a way to shut my good mood down and make me miserable. It's simple things such as conversations where I don't think before I speak or my sarcasm slips when I don't mean to let the venom free. Or when I try to grow a peaceful garden in my mind, they let the locusts loose to consume my freshly bloomed flowers to where my mind is just an empty, desolate wasteland with no chance of escape or reprieve.

My mind remains in a state of Disturbia that freely lets monsters roam and suck out what bit of vitality I have. The monsters come in all shapes, sizes, and disguises. It can be words taken out of context that weren't meant or be hostile or even a memory that brings forth the pain, the anger, the anguish, or even despair. They create a blackened labyrinth that offers no hope that the end of the maze is near. They just toss out obstacles that lead me astray from the path I should be walking, ultimately damaging me more in the end.

Dear Diary,

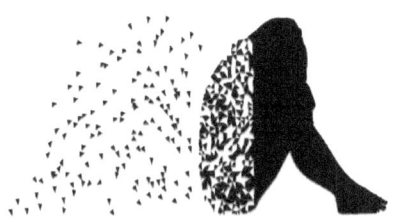

I was a caged bird born to a volatile mother and alcoholic, drug-addled father, and they locked me away as if I were a princess. However, a princess wasn't a grand thing to be. I was a princess of proportions that Disney had never written about. Sure, Snow White's stepmother tried to kill her. But her villain was her stepmother, and Snow White was blissfully unaware of how evil her stepmother was.

I'm not sure what or if my mother had ever been diagnosed with any type of mental health instabilities, but I know now she should have been, and if she had, she should have taken her medication appropriately. She was physically, mentally, emotionally, and verbally abusive on varying levels, and the degree of abuse was subjective to what throttled it.

I'm not sure at what point my father started doing drugs, but I know for a fact it was happening when I was in high school, if not in elementary school, no matter how oblivious my family tried to keep me from the secret. His alcoholism was nothing new to me. He had been a daily drinker for years, but there were times I can remember as a child that instead of cracking a beer with meals, he had a glass of Pepsi with ice. At some point, that glass of Pepsi changed into a beer, and then that beer turned into liquor.

There was this one time I firmly remember not being able to come home because he was in a drunken, high rage sick with pneumonia from snorting pills that were coated in a gel to prevent drug addicts from using them, threatening to kill my mother and needing to calm down. I was at an audition for the talent show in high school and stayed after to watch my niece in her track meet, catching a ride home with my brother. They wouldn't allow me to go home and didn't tell me anything until we had arrived at their house, right next to mine. When I was finally able to go up to the house, he was still drunk and talking shit to my mom. He was like that, though.

There were multitudes of times his narcissistic personality broke through. Once, my mother had taken me shopping in the city. We spent nearly all day out that day shopping for school clothes and supplies and all after her doctor's appointment. When we got home, and I was going through the things we bought, he came in yelling at me for not cleaning the kitchen. I hadn't been home all day to do my chores. I was also on my period with very painful cramps. Add that to the stress of being yelled at over something that wasn't my fault. I had my first panic attack. At the time, we didn't know what I experienced was a panic attack. It felt more like a food allergy. I couldn't breathe. I felt like I was dying. I itched everywhere and scratching only made my body feel like Jello. I couldn't walk. I couldn't talk. I was even tested for seizures because the symptoms of panic attacks mimicked seizures along with food allergies. Those who have seizures that aren't epileptic are said to have pseudo-seizures that PTSD causes. After many years of experiencing these situations, it all came bubbling to the surface in a PTSD panic attack that I still have to this day. My therapist has brought up that even those panic attacks may be pseudo-seizures, but for now, we are sticking to panic attacks as we delve deeper into my trauma.

It wasn't my father alone abusing me. My mother was the physical abuser, the mental and emotional abuser. I was a bed wetter up through my teenage years. I would be punished for wetting the bed. Punishment ranged, too, depending on the type of mood she was in. Once, she handed me a cup and told me she had wrung the piss from my sheets and demanded I drink the liquid to teach me a lesson for wetting the bed. Even though the cup was full of salt water, I believed the liquid to be what my mother said as a naive seven-year-old. Sometimes, she made me wear diapers to bed. There was a particularly mortifying experience when I came home from school one day, and we had a guest over that she led to my room. She asked me where the diaper was. I had stuffed it under my bed because I feared punishment. She berated me in front of a man who was my brother's friend over wetting the bed. She made me wear them to school when I was in fourth grade. I had a leakage issue, and she didn't believe me that I wasn't peeing on myself in school because I came home smelling like urine. She had told me she hoped my friends knew what I was wearing, and then maybe I would stop embarrassing her with my bed-wetting. That's just the tip of the iceberg.

Growing up, I thought what happened to me was normal. I thought all kids were punished the same way I had been. My mom got pregnant with me because she was lonely. It took her six years to conceive me because my father was never home. He was always out at a bar he ran with my grandpa, getting drunk. They lived in a rundown house. Well, you couldn't call the abomination a house. What they called a trailer, or a house, was a shack with a dirt floor, no electricity, or running water. A nail kept the door shut, and my mom had to tote gallons of water from her parents' house to ours to take baths and wash dishes. She had lost her mother three years prior to my birth and was very depressed and even suicidal herself. Pair that with the loneliness of feeling like a single parent because your husband was either never home or always drinking, and you feel utterly alone. I myself have experienced that feeling numerous times throughout my marriage. Most likely, it is another instance of where my mother's life molded what type of life I had.

I'm not a total monster. I sympathize with my mother and what she went through prior to my birth, but we moved when I was a baby. Things were better. We had an actual trailer. We had power. We had water. We had food. Her life had gotten better, and I can empathize with this because I experienced the same thing when I moved from the rundown home I had inherited from them and into the house my husband and I had bought with our own money. But having nice things doesn't stop depression or any type of mental illness.

It would take many years to learn that in the 80s and 90s, mental illness was taboo. My mother's sister was diagnosed schizophrenic in the 80s. My mother didn't want to be looked at the same way her sister was; consequently, she hid her depression, her anxiety, and her other undiagnosed mental illnesses. Court systems, childcare systems, schools, and every other infrastructure frowned upon parents who weren't mentally stable. So, my mother hid her issues in the same way I did. But you would think the similarities between us would make her more compassionate or more empathetic when her own children started to present with the same mental instability that she had suffered. It did not, and I still suffer from her lack of motherly concern.

The thought of dying had crossed my mind numerous times throughout my childhood. I always felt like I should have never been born, that my birth caused some form of ripple effect that changed my family. I wasn't allowed to go outside and play like normal children. I wasn't allowed to have friends over. I wasn't allowed to do anything except clean the house.

Sometimes, one of my brothers would take me with them to the movies, or we would go to a comic book shop where they played RPG card games. Freedom. But all good things never last long, and that soon stopped as well when he and his wife started having marital issues. So, I was once again trapped in a house that never felt like home to me. When I started middle school, my life became a nightmare. I went to school and caught verbal abuse from bullies and would come home to be bullied as well. This soon began to wear away at my fragile spirit. One day, that spirit broke. My mom hadn't washed clothes all week for me to go to school. I had two pieces of clothing that didn't even match, but I didn't and couldn't miss school. So, I wore the horribly mismatched outfit to school, and my classmates didn't miss a beat snickering about the ensemble or talking about my clothes behind my back and loud enough for me to hear.

The thought of dying wasn't a thought that was new at all to me. Suicidal ideation wasn't a foreign concept as I had stood many times in the kitchen while cleaning as my mother slept away on the couch and my father drank his beer watching TV in his own living room while I clutched my mother's pills in my hand trying to work up the courage to swallow the whole bottle. The one positive thing about moments like that was I was alone, but I was also a danger to myself. I remember holding a bottle of my mother's muscle relaxers as tears streamed down my face, wishing for the courage to down the entire bottle and drift off into sweet oblivion. I had stared at her bottles before, wondering if they would work or if I would just be in trouble for trying to end the pain I cycled through. I had played with her valium bottle. I had tinkered around with her pain pill bottle. But I was never brave enough to crack the lid and down them by the handfuls until I felt numb, until I felt the exhaustion leave my body, and the fatigue let me drift off into darkness.

But that day at school, where I was not only just bullied by the normal group of boys but by everyone in my classes, I made my decision. I had heard what people always said about me. I was fat. I was ugly. I was worthless. No one would ever love me the way I was. No one would ever choose me the way I was. No one to me was everyone, even though there were people that did care about me. I wrote one of those people my note. I wasn't going to leave one to find at home. I was just going to go home, swipe the bottle of pills, and slip off into my room. They'd only come to check on me to yell at me to do my chores. I gave my note to my best and what felt like my only friend at the time. And she lost it.

She left the room after speaking with the teacher in tears. And when she returned, she returned with an adult that pulled me from class. I knew what she did. She told on me. I expected the experience to be more dramatic than what the experience really turned out to be. The person she told was our school counselor. I don't even think she reported the incident to the principal because there were just the two of us in the room while we spoke.

In my first diary entry, I briefly went over all of this, but I realized I needed to get the whole story out. I need to say everything to cope with what happened to me. Even if it's just words on paper, they're my words, and I need to bleed those words out before I bleed myself out.

"Why did you write this note?" she asked me.

I sat there silently, shrugging my shoulders. I had never spoken to anyone about my abuse, and the last time my sister did, her telling adults didn't do any good. So why should I tell her? And then she asked the million-dollar question.

"Why are you depressed?" No, I take that back. She didn't ask why I was depressed. See, that's the misconception with questions nowadays. There are a myriad of ways to read into a question and find ulterior questions within a question. Her real question... why was I unhappy? What made me unhappy? Why did I want to kill myself?

And I stared at her. How was I to answer that question when it's a million things but nothing at the same time? Yes, I had experienced abuse and trauma. My grandfather had died not too long before I hit the bottom. I wasn't even that close to him. For most of my childhood, he was bedridden from a stroke, unable to speak properly. It was a terrifying experience whenever we would go over, and I would see him in his hospital bed. He had lost his legs from bed sores and gangrene that developed from being in a bed all the time. The infection wasn't exactly treatable because he had diabetes, which made healing sores a complication. But that was one of my answers.

When I am put under pressure, I can't speak. My anxiety rages, and I can't find the words to say what is wrong with me. Most of the time, I just sob. It's the only thing I know how to do. The pressure of this counselor wanting to know why I was depressed flared my anxiety. So, instead of telling her about my abuse, I told her my grandfather had just died. The grief of his death did floor me. I cried for days, and I sank into a black hole. But that moment wasn't the first time I had felt this way, and I didn't feel safe telling that to a person I barely knew.

"What else makes you feel this way?" she asked.

My heart raced. How could I explain this? Does anyone know how to explain this? Adults are asked this question time and time again by people who do not understand mental illness. It's evident now how taboo the idea of mental health disorders is in today's society. There are always answers from people like, "Oh, you don't think I am depressed? I still get shit done." Or "You're just sad. Do something that makes you happy." Or "Just get over it." I didn't want anything of the sort thrown back at me.

"A lot of things," is what I told her, like my parents yelling at me for not doing my chores right. The pressure from school. I had received an F on my report card. I had never had an F, ever, and the timing was when my grandfather died. The teacher claimed I never turned in my paper when I had witnesses that saw me leave it on her desk. I still received an F, and the grade bothered me. If I didn't have the grades in school, I couldn't escape my life by going to college.

I told her how everything just felt wrong in my life. I felt like I didn't belong anywhere. People at school were mean to me. She made me sign a piece of paper promising I wouldn't harm myself at home, which is really fucking stupid. What would my punishment have been had I not gone through with my promise? I signed the paper, went back to class, and finished my day. She called my mom and told her about the note. I know I have spoken about my mother's reaction toward me, but there wasn't as much detail as I recall now. When I got home, I was bombarded with anger. She had found a story I had been writing about a girl, a former diary, who was depressed and suicidal after looking through my room once she got off the phone with the counselor.

"Why would you write this?" she demanded.

"I don't know," I replied quietly.

My sister stood beside her with tears in her eyes. My sister cared about what I had written. My sister was not mad. My sister was not angry. My sister worried about me. I would find out much later that she, too, had grappled with depression, and our mother told her to be quiet about how she felt and refused her therapy because she didn't like what she was telling the therapist, which explains why my mother said what she did to me.

"Do you want to go live with other people? Do you want me to look like a bad mother? Because that is exactly what you are doing. They will take you away and put you with strangers to live. Don't say it ever again."

And that was that. My mother never prodded further to see why I was depressed, to see why I was broken. She never took me to the doctor for depression medication. She never took me to a therapist to see why her thirteen-year-old daughter was suicidal. She never brought the issue up again. And that still hurts today. Why couldn't she hug me? Why couldn't she cry for me? Why couldn't she cry with me? Why couldn't she tell me she loved me? Why couldn't she tell me everything would be ok? That she would make life better for me? Why couldn't she be a mother? She wore the title proudly and told everyone her children were her whole world, but when her daughters stood before her, broken and beaten down by her, by the world, by themselves, she was narcissistic and turned their valid feelings around on them. She was worried about what people would think of her, what people would say about her.

Why weren't we as important as she claimed us to be?

It was in moments like this that sparked the question of who loves me, and when I had no secure answer, the question switched to who would love me. I questioned the very essence of my own mother's care for me. My mother would tell me she loved me, not very often, but still told me, but her actions proved otherwise to my subconscious. Couple that with my socially inept life from bullies at school, and I was a walking poster child for the unwanted and unclaimed.

This tied together several undiagnosed mental instabilities such as mild agoraphobia, anthropophobia (a fear of people), philophobia (a fear of love), and severe crippling social anxiety. I spent the majority of the pandemic locked away in my house. We hardly even went to family's houses to visit. I had tried being more social with my family; thus, we started venturing out to see people more and more during the pandemic. However, I was hit with back-to-back panic attacks not long after being around the area where I grew up. The house that we had abandoned and moved from was the very house I grew up in. Once I stopped going back to it, I felt like something lifted.

I live far enough out where surprise visits from anyone aren't an issue. I left my past in the past, and I could feel a difference in myself. Several members of my husband's family have suggested we move back, but I defiantly say no. My childhood traumas were in that house. Pair those traumas with the fact the house was also where my mom died, traumatizing me further because I witnessed her death, and I felt at peace not being there anymore.

The walls of that house are a constant reminder of my prison life as a child. A lot of the time we spent there, I had no escape from the place. I stayed there alone with my children while my husband worked out of town, and those years were the loneliest period of my life. In those moments, I felt exactly how my mother had felt prior to my birth. I was spiraling with my mental health. My mother-in-law had passed. I was having marital problems. I had a newborn baby along with my other two children I had to care for alone, sometimes for weeks at a time. Then, my father passed. I had plenty of emotional baggage hitting me all at once, and I hit a dark place. I had no support system. I had no way to find a support system because I had no transportation.

I would usually spend my time going to my nephew's house right down the street from me and taking the kids so they could play with his daughters. His mom lived with him; therefore, I had someone to talk to. Drugs became an issue with him, and soon he was strung out with the multitude of people affected by the meth and heroin crisis that was hitting our hometown. His mother moved out of the house, and I was once again alone. I wasn't sleeping properly and suffering from insomnia. I felt like a mental case, and my mental instability wasn't solely affecting me but my children as well. I was oversleeping, and my daughter was missing school.

I hit the darkest period I had ever felt. The darkness was deeper than when I was thirteen, and I left that note for my friend. I started to slip into that numb feeling where the grief and despair no longer hurt because I couldn't feel anything. One night, I sat in the bathtub with a razor to my wrist, asking an online friend if it would be horrible of me to just end my life right then and there. They, too, had experienced what I experienced. We bonded over our dark plights and were each other's support system when we had no one to turn to. They told me if I was going to commit suicide, I didn't need to do it because of how others made me feel like I had to. If I were going to do the act, do it because I was setting myself free of my own torment and not to appease how others felt about me not being worthy. I pressed the razor against my wrist and was about to slice when I heard my baby cry in the room down the hall. That cry was my light in the dark. That cry told me that I had people who depended on me at that moment. That cry told me I was wanted and needed. That cry told me that there was someone in the house that loved me. My children loved me.

My children didn't see me as the warped reflection I saw of myself. They didn't see me as ugly or fat. They saw me as their mother and loved me unconditionally. They were my wake-up call. I set the razor down and went to the room. I did my motherly duty with a swollen heart and cried myself to sleep. That house had nearly claimed my soul not once, not twice, but multifarious times. People in my life and places in my life were triggers to my mental health. How do you work around a trigger when it's an actual person from your family? How do you explain that you don't want to be around people from your family because it's a reminder of your past traumas without being judged for it? How do you tell your family that you hate your parents for what they did to you?

I mentioned I had philophobia, a fear of love, but I don't go into detail about it. I want love. I want to be loved. I want to drown in love, and I have drowned in love. That is why I fear love immensely. I am so starved for affection that I put my entire soul into people and care about them, whether that affection is fully reciprocated or not. I then overthink every single little thing. What if they don't really love me? What if I am the only one who loves them, and I am just an obligation to be fulfilled? My mother always said they would never love me because I was fat. So, I also push people away while intrusive thoughts take over my mind and whisper horrible things that echo from my past. I hardly have close friends and the ones I do live miles and miles away from me in other states where they can't hurt me in real life. My one solid relationship has been riddled with pain and heartbreak but also with love and light that those thoughts are extremely unbearable to think that he doesn't love me the way I love him. So, there is a vicious cycle of me being completely clingy and then pushing him away because I don't feel as if my love is accepted the way love should be, or I let every little thing he has ever said eat away at me while I sit and obsess over the past. I honestly feel like I am a broken lightbulb that keeps flickering on and off with light, and I don't know how to keep the coil from completely burning up and submerging me into a blanket of total darkness.

I see multitudes of people say to embrace the darkness, and I have been one of those people, too. But the darkness that threatens to suffocate me is piles of blankets when I'm not too fond of blankets touching my face. That darkness is a bitter and numb suppressant that eats away at my insides like cancer growing and metastasizing. It is dangerous to me because the darkness is where reality halts. This altered state of reality is not peaceful for me but traumatizing and agonizing because I am all alone in that space. Darkness is where the demons lie in wait for me to become vulnerable, and I fight tooth and nail to stay out on the outskirts of the shadows. If I let blankets succumb too quickly, I can't escape the abyss. I must always be aware of its existence because if that inky black hole sneaks up on me and catches me unaware, I feel like it's too late for me to fight the rising waters that threaten to drown me in the well I have tumbled down. I don't know how to swim. I was never taught, and when my feet can't touch the bottom, I panic. I panic in the abysmal inky blackness of my mind and fear that whatever I am ferrying across the swamp of misery will capsize. So, I stay close to the shore. I won't wade into the deep waters where pockets of quicksand hidden beneath the decaying debris can pull me under, where mouthfuls of air turn into mouthfuls of mud, and I can no longer breathe. I need to breathe!

Dear Diary,

What constitutes abuse? At what point does discipline become abuse? Is the one time a parent loses control abuse? Is a red mark left from a hand abuse? Does the situation matter if a belt or a paddle was used to whip you instead of a hand? At what point does the moment go from being disciplined to being abused? What makes the experience abuse? And how many times does everything need to happen before the discipline is called child abuse? Just once? Multiple times? What if the parent beat the kid one time, and that was all? Is that abuse? Even as an adult, I grapple with calling what I experienced child abuse.

I always feel as if the rest of my family was okay with the treatment we received from our mother and father. I feel as if they think the way I do with my fucked-up sense of a warped reality. What happened to me wasn't bad. What happened to me was normal. What happened to me wasn't child abuse. Our parents bought me things. If I wanted something, most of the time, I got what I wanted. Some would call me spoiled, just like my siblings believed I was. To them, I was a spoiled brat who didn't listen to our parents even though they gave me everything they thought I wanted. They were jealous because when they lived there, we didn't have the money like we did after they left. It wasn't like my parents didn't give them money, but that wasn't the point.

I didn't want nice things. I wanted my mom to come to my choir performances. I wanted to be able to play soccer. I wanted to be able to do extracurricular activities. My mom or my sister would usually drop me off and pick me up from my performances instead of sitting there and watching me. I was good. I was good enough that my choir teacher wanted me to perform the Star-Spangled Banner at the basketball games, but Mom wouldn't let me. I wasn't allowed to go to games after school because it was an inconvenience for her time.

There was this one time when I auditioned and earned a spot in the drama performance for school. The only way I could do that after-school activity was if I had a ride after school, which I did. I had a friend who would bring me home until one day, she couldn't because they needed to do something after practice. I called my mother and asked if she could pick me up, and she flat out told me no, that I needed to find a ride home or walk, an instance of actual abandonment and anxiety I had firsthand. Something I could have forgone had I had my license. I didn't get a license until I was 18. I had held a learner's permit since I was 16, but my mother wouldn't give me the hours required for a licensed person to ride with me. By eighteen, I had held my learner's permit so long I didn't need to turn in a form to verify my hours. Her excuse was her anxiety couldn't handle me driving, and no one else stepped up to help me get my hours.

Luckily, my now sister-in-law was sitting there, and I was able to get her to come and get me as the sky was nearly dusk outside, which would have meant walking nearly ten miles home in the dark down a winding back country road. That day was my last practice, and I had to drop out of the drama production because I didn't have reliable transportation. All of this was inconvenient to my mother, and I just wanted to feel loved and appreciated for what I was accomplishing, just like my middle brother. He played football, and she went to his games to cheer him on, but I never had anyone there to cheer me on. I never had anyone or got to experience anything growing up.

I wanted family time outside of the holidays. I wanted family vacations. I wanted things from them that money couldn't buy. I wanted time. I wanted experience. I wanted joy and happiness. I didn't want to be bought things. I wanted love, affection, and attention. I wanted what I felt starved for because I loved my parents deeply but didn't understand the whys of it all.

My entire family chastised me for being a bedwetter. I stopped seeing a doctor for the condition when I was in elementary school. They tried pills. They tried the beeping mat that I couldn't even hear in my sleep. I was sixteen before I stopped. There are times, even as an adult, I have woken up to soiled underwear, having to rush to the bathroom to finish because I was under extreme stress and anxiety. Waking up wet is just as mortifying now as it was then.

On occasion, my sister would come and get me to spend the weekend at her house, but the time away from home was never without consequence. Even staying somewhere else, I didn't escape the mental abuse because our mother had also warped my sister. I was still a bed wetter, and she reminded me of how disgusting and embarrassing it was for her sister to wet the bed in her boyfriend's house. Well, I should say wet the floor because I wasn't allowed to sleep on anything I could piss on. I pushed her callous words out of thought and out of mind because I had freedom at my sister's house. When she took me to Florida with her on vacation when I was fifteen, she scolded me every morning I woke up, and there were wet sheets that needed to be cleaned.

I was whipped with a paddle for wetting the bed throughout elementary school. It's an inherited trait because my mother was twelve before she stopped, and I have a cousin who was a full adult still urinating in his sleep on my mom's side. That fact did not stop the abuse around my bed wetting and being punished for something I couldn't control, only prolonged it. My oldest child was a bedwetter, and I didn't make a big deal out of it. I was a bed wetter; thus, naturally, one of my kids would be. When she was nine, I took her to the doctor just to prove a point that it was genetic. The doctor agreed and said any type of anxiety surrounding her bed-wetting issues wouldn't help and would prolong her bed-wetting. I never once criticized her for nightly accidents. I never once punished her for wetting the bed because I knew what that felt like. We bought her plastic bed protectors, and she chose to wear pull-ups to bed. By 10, she had stopped.

I have always wished I had been born into a different family and had a different life. Not one where secrets are claimed to be lies, and then more lies are poured on top of those secrets to make them seem as if they weren't true. Like my sister accusing me of killing our mother just because I said I was abused in a Facebook post and was lying because "she was there." She was never there. And the few times she was there to witness my abuse, she let the abuse happen. But saying my experiences of being backed into a wall and being wailed on over and over is a lie, and then saying I was the cause of our mother dying really broke me. I have no family. I have always felt like an orphan, and now I am an orphan.

When my mom had her stroke, I was in my last year of college. Just days prior, I had gotten into an argument with my dad because I hadn't cleaned when my mother paid my cousin to clean the house with an oxycontin pill for his habit. He took the pill and didn't clean. I was hardly home. I had classes that went on all day. But since, and I quote my father, I lived there free, I needed to clean his house. Even though my cousin lived there for free as well, on the run from his arrest warrant for skipping out on his jail sentence because he had sold pills for my dad and got caught by the person where a wire during the transaction, it was still solely my duty as it had always been since my sister moved out. I was moving out when she had her stroke and actively searching for a cheap apartment to pay rent for near my school.

Dear Diary,

When I was in middle school, things started to change around my house, and I had no clue what it was about. My mom started sleeping on the couch. My dad was spending more and more time out of town, and I didn't know why. I started to venture out of my room more during this time. Broadband internet had become a new thing, and we had internet installed in the house; therefore, I spent a good amount of time online while my mother slept or my dad was gone. This turned into a long-term thing. I didn't know why he had to go out of town all the time. He wasn't working. Both of my parents were disabled. But the older I got, the more and more he wasn't home. Christmas came with more gifts that were expensive. My mom developed a habit of shopping on eBay and bought exceedingly large amounts of stuff off there.

I grew up knowing we were poor. Being on disability meant you were poor. I had no idea how much my parents made for disability, but apparently, they made enough money to do all these things. I was completely oblivious to the fact that we really weren't poor. We were poor on paper. Off paper, we were well off. It wasn't until I had graduated high school that I learned how we were poor off paper. Not only was my father addicted to the pain pills that he was prescribed, but he got that way by selling them. He was an oxycontin kingpin for West Virginia and Ohio, and the best dealers always showed their customers how good the product was.

When I had stopped wetting the bed, my mom started letting me sleep in her room, and she would sleep in there as well. This became a habit. I guess she was lonely and didn't want to sleep in there alone because until my dad had started going out of town, they slept in the same bed together. After a while, my dad told me he and my mother not sleeping in their bed together was my fault. He said he couldn't sleep in his own bed because I was sleeping in it, which affected his marriage with my mother. So, I stopped sleeping in there. They still slept on their own respective couches in their separate living rooms whenever he was in town. Mom slept on the couch whether he was home or not toward the end of my high school years.

Dear Diary,

I have a predisposition to addiction. I have mentioned this once before, but I don't think people truly understand what I mean. One of the forms of self-harm in victims of child abuse and neglect is drugs and alcohol to cope with their mental illnesses that stem from the abuse or to cope with the memories and the PTSD. Mental illnesses can cause an addiction issue just by making the person feel alive and euphoric, showing them the upside of doing drugs and linking to an internal need for the substance because the chemical composition corrects their off-kilter brain chemicals. That need is a part of mental illness, and mental illness runs rampant in my family. But what ran even more rampant was drug and alcohol addiction.

I can feel the tingle in my body whenever I think of illicit drugs or alcohol. I can feel the warmth of liquor roll across my tongue and tastebuds, then slide down my throat into my stomach and warmth spread across my body. I can feel the high of snorting a pill or smoking meth and the elation those substances bring at canceling the noise in my head. I feel every part of addiction, and my body craves the release, but I do not give in.

Not only is my brain hardwired for a driving force of causing an addiction when the drugs feel good, but my exposure to drugs and alcohol, paired with child abuse and self-destructive behaviors, also predisposed me to a life of addiction. I fight that every single day. I am aware of the addiction. I am aware of what happens with addiction, and I fight every single day to not become an addict because addiction is ingrained in me through brain chemistry and by witnessing the use of drugs firsthand being okay by adults who were supposed to protect me. But those of us who fight against the temptation instead of giving in aren't considered addicts or get recognition for fighting the urge instead of giving into the chemical release, knowing the consequences.

I see people post on social media all the time that if you have never been addicted to anything, you don't have a right to an opinion about those who have given into drugs and addiction and getting clean. Even those who are recovering addicts do not see people as addicts or a recovering addict just because they fought the urge to lean into darkness instead of giving into the same urge and having to journey the same way they did, learning lessons.

Do we have to go to meetings in order to be considered an addict? My name is Christine Jane Addison, and I am an addict. I have never let myself get lost in the urge of drugs and alcohol, although I do occasionally partake. I know that if I lost control of my thoughts and my actions, I would spiral down the rabbit hole of addiction; hence, I choose not to lose control. But that temptation to do the very thing that killed my father and nephew is there every day because the idea sounds extremely blissful to let go. You would let go of your worries, your fears, and your inhibitions and be free of the monster trapped inside of you because you can't think of trauma when you're on cloud nine while feeding an even bigger monster that refuses to let go. But just because I have never gotten lost in drugs does not mean I am not an addict if I know what my future looks like with daily use. I have witnessed what addiction does to a family. I lived it. I deserve an opinion on recovering addicts because just because I didn't have a physical addiction, I have a mental addiction, and it's just as bad as if I were an addict.

Mental addiction has a formal name in mental health. Substance abuse disorder. I have compulsive eating issues. I have compulsive actions. The compulsive consumption of substances, knowing the consequences, is in my blood, and I fight it. Fighting addiction doesn't mean you have to fight after starting drugs. Fighting addiction can be fought just because you know what will happen if you do it. Case in point, my nephew grew up aware of drug abuse in the family. He turned to drugs when things got hard in his life, knowing that he would have an addiction issue because addiction is throughout the family. His mom was an addict. His grandpa was an addict. His grandpa's family are addicts. His argument was he could quit whenever he wanted to. He was already addicted when he said those words. He already triggered the same compulsive consumption button we all have because addiction is a mental health instability that runs in our family. He is in his second attempt at sobriety, and I hope he overcomes it. His brother was also an addict. He has been clean for six years.

It's just as big an accomplishment to choose to stay sober as it is for an addict to get sober when you come from a family of addicts and alcoholics. So, if you celebrate every day that you didn't decide to give into a family curse... me too. We all have demons that call for that release.

Since I was in elementary school, age range of nine to eleven, my mom would let me have my own beer. She liked the Zima drinks, and I was allowed to have my own and drink with her whenever she would buy them. It was when I was around seventeen or eighteen years old that my mom started drinking in excess. She wasn't a raging alcoholic, but she did drink every single day. She didn't have anyone to drink with; ergo, she let me drink with her. Every night, we had drinks. Before I ever hit twenty-one, I was getting drunk with my mom. It wasn't unusual at that point. When she started waking up in the mornings and making pina coladas or strawberry daiquiris marked the point that her drinking became a problem. My middle brother commented to her about the alcohol not being good, especially with her heart condition. On the days I didn't have school, I would drink with her for company, but there were many times I had to turn down daiquiris at 8 am.

After she died, I started drinking more. I got blitzed for my 21st birthday. Whenever there was an opportunity to drink, I was doing it. I would drink if I were happy. I would drink if I were unhappy. I hardly ever drink now. I don't want to be an alcoholic. I don't want to have a need for alcohol. I don't want to have a need for drugs; therefore, I don't particularly appreciate taking pain prescriptions when given to me. Once I had my hysterectomy and the pain lasted for longer than intended, I got another script of pain meds from the doctor for another ten days. My healing was slow because I was diabetic. When I was still in pain, I asked for another prescription, but instead, I asked for a non-narcotic pain prescription. I didn't want to become addicted to the same thing that is the big family secret. I've tried cocaine before, and it wasn't really for me. The amped-up feeling made my anxiety worse.

Dear Diary,

The first time I ever smoked weed, I was twenty-one, standing with my sister on her front porch. That side effect that almost everyone experiences hit me: the munchies. And for once in my life, I wasn't afraid to eat whatever I wanted to eat. Marijuana causes a euphoric feeling and lowers your inhibitions. It relaxes you and calms you. However, cannabis was still "taboo" where I lived; thus, I didn't smoke a lot. I smoked once or twice here and there and then stopped completely when I got a job and a month later found out I was pregnant. After my first pregnancy ended with a miscarriage, I began to smoke weed once a day.

I was back living with my dad, and he was gone all the time like he had always been while growing up, off selling his pills. I basically lived alone for the first time in my life. I ended up pregnant again. I tested four days earlier than recommended, and the pregnancy test was positive; ergo, I quit smoking. I was a rollercoaster of emotions. I know a lot of people put the emotional aspect off on pregnancy hormones, but I noticed a clear difference in myself while smoking weed. I let go of my inhibitions and worries, fears. I could eat food without feeling like I shouldn't be eating it, and I didn't have guilt and shame after, either. I felt my depression ease away and my anxiety lift some. And then I ended up pregnant with my first born.

I didn't start back after either because I had a newborn to care for. I tried breastfeeding first, and then after, I couldn't breastfeed because I didn't want to eat a lot of food and get fat after losing weight during pregnancy. I didn't produce the milk. I would smoke here and there, but not enough to treat myself. I had a job, and I couldn't risk getting drug tested and fired because recreational use was still illegal in my state. I completely stopped smoking because the effects would linger after. When I went to work, I felt like everyone knew I was high, which, in turn, ramped up my anxiety and paranoia. Plus, this job had the possibility of getting hurt on the job, and I was paying my own bills and couldn't go back to living with my husband's toxic family again.

At this point, my father had permanently moved to West Virginia. I had no support system or fallback people. Not to mention, there was tension between us after an incident with my husband. I had to rely on myself for me, my husband, and my child to survive. It would be after my third miscarriage before I smoked weed enough again to treat myself. But once again, I ended up pregnant and stopped smoking to rinse and repeat. This time was a harder transition for me. As I have mentioned before, my mother-in-law died, I had marital problems, I had a new baby, and my father died.

By the middle of 2018, I decided to medicate again using weed. My husband was the one working, so I didn't have to worry about the risk of getting fired. I needed to escape the chronic loneliness I felt due to him being out of town. However, I was forced into seeing a therapist and psychiatrist and told to stop medicating with marijuana and try medications again. I had been on three different medications throughout the years to this point.

In 2019, I started Topamax. The medication was horrible. I ended up with serotonin syndrome. I lost my sense of taste. I became erratic and even more manic than I was before. The medication completely exacerbated all my mental illness symptoms. I was on it for a month before my psychiatrist changed it from that to Lithium. That one messed with my kidneys, and my legs and feet began to swell; consequently, I was switched off that medication and onto Ambien. At this point, my anxiety was tremendously bad from all the medications. I needed what I had been on before for anxiety and that Xanax or Klonopin. However, the facility I went to refused to use scheduled narcotics in their program since voluminous amounts of the patients were addicts. Instead, they gave me medication that was like anxiety medication but didn't treat my anxiety.

I started to lie to the psychiatrist and stopped taking all my medication. Everything I tried didn't work and only made me feel worse. I tried out Ambien for a good six months before I stopped taking it. Once I was out of court-ordered visitation, I stopped going altogether.

Why did I put myself through all the torture? Two reasons: 1) I had to because the court ordered me into psychiatric help. 2) I was having marital problems and wanted to fix me because I was the problem. My mental illness was the reason we were in the situation we were currently in. We argued every day, which worsened my mental health. We both wanted to call our marriage quits, but we had our kids to think about.

Dear Diary,

During the times I lived with my dad after having no choice but to live with him, those days were extremely lonely and exhausting. I hardly got to see my husband, who at the time was just my boyfriend and future baby daddy. I was put back into the role I had always had. Cook, clean, and wait on my dad like a servant. After I had gotten pregnant with my oldest child, I was allowed to go back around my now in-laws' house again. I spent every chance I could spending time with my husband. My brother had given us a trailer to repair and set up to move into. I had plans of living on my own.

During this time, my father was sick with the flu or from snorting the gel-coated pills again. I was spending the day with my husband. My father had slipped and fell while I was gone, and my brother called me angry that I wasn't there taking care of him. I didn't know it had become my responsibility to care for him like I had my mother. My oldest brother said I lived there, and it was my duty to make sure everything in the house was spick and span so my dad didn't have issues getting around. Once again, I wasn't the only one living there. My cousin lived there as well. As far as I could tell, he helped my dad get around. So, I told him I wasn't living there because, honestly, the house was just a place to stay until I could move into a place of my own.

After my comment, my brother took my dad to West Virginia and boarded/locked up the house to where I couldn't stay there anymore since I wasn't "living there." I have always had to work to earn my keep everywhere. In order for me to stay in the house, I had to care for my father as I did my mother, even though I had a life for once. How is it that it had become my sole responsibility to take care of both of my parents. I was young, too young. I was only twenty-two by this time. We had another sibling that lived on the property, our middle brother, since my oldest brother lived in West Virginia. From that point, I hardly saw my dad ever again. He was in the hospital for a while and then lived with my brother in West Virginia.

My dad had given me access to his bank account to use the forty dollars that was direct deposited from his SSI into there. After a while, I was talking to my dad on the phone when he told me my brother didn't want me using the checkbook anymore because I was fucking up his finances. I had been using the forty dollars to buy food here and there for me to eat because my husband's parents were always broken and couldn't afford to feed everyone living there, and my food stamps for myself didn't last long because I was feeding everyone there. My dad was apologetic for asking, but I handed over the checkbook willingly because I was not using him for his money. I always asked if I could spend the money before using it.

I was always seen as a moocher whenever I would ask for money to help me get by as we struggled. A couple of hundred dollars once, twenty here or twenty there is hardly being a moocher compared to the hundreds of thousands of dollars my father had given my siblings throughout the years. But I didn't matter because no one liked my husband since he didn't have a job to take care of us. We made ends meet with him scrapping metal, and then I got a job that would carry us until he got a job. He was still looked down upon because I was the one supporting us and not him.

There was one incident that left the family angry at both of us when he stole rings to pawn to put food on the table when we had been living with my father when he returned to Virginia. My oldest was still a baby, and once again, the food stamps were feeding more people than allotted. My father was buying pills to feed his addiction rather than buying food. My husband was trying to sell meat for a living and was wasting more money on gas than he earned. My dad pressed charges against him, and he went to jail for a month. Everyone had stolen from my dad. My cousin living with us had stolen hundreds if not thousands of dollars from him to feed his own addiction, but my husband was the villain. My dad even accused me of being in on the theft because that's what the detective had told him, and he chose not to press charges against me. The accusation was all a lie because I had no idea he had stolen from my dad. It wasn't until the day of court, when I saw his signature on the pawn slip, that I realized he had done it. He even called me from jail apologizing, fearing I didn't want to be with him because he had really stolen his ring and confessed to me, which I told him I knew. But I also knew what he did with the money that I had thought he had gotten selling meat.

My father left to live with my brother in West Virginia again after this. The one parent that had always abandoned me was him. He was never there after I hit middle school. He wasn't there while I was living with him because he was off selling pills. So, I became stuck once again in an abusive household with my in-laws, who didn't like me and made it known they didn't like me. At one point, right before we had moved in to live with my dad, I had gotten into a literal fistfight with my mother-in-law and brother-in-law after arguing with my brother-in-law. We had made a little money doing some side work, and my husband had paid $50 on the light bill, and then we went out for dinner for his birthday. My husband and brother-in-law began to argue when he tried to bust the windshield out of the truck, then came inside to start in on how useless I was living

46

there. We put food in the house, and we also let my husband's parents claim us on taxes to make up for any money we didn't provide in the house outside of my husband doing side jobs and scrapping to feed people.

I had enough and was in the middle of packing when she stormed in to tell me to pack my shit and get out, to which I yelled that was what I was doing. She charged at me, and I pushed her back into the hallway because I didn't want her hitting me, and I didn't want to hit her. My brother-in-law came in from behind me and punched me in the head. It was all touch and go at that point until my father-in-law heard the commotion from outside. All I remember is the door opening and the light coming in from outside as he pulled her outside, leaving me with my brother-in-law, who was choking me. I was gouging his eyes when he returned, picked my brother-in-law up, and threw him across the room because they were doing this in front of my seven-month-old baby.

After my husband went to jail, I moved back in with them because I couldn't be alone with my dad again, especially after he had accused me of being a thief as well. My husband and I got married the day he got out of jail. I got a job during this time and was putting money into the house and buying things for the house, to which his brother still complained wasn't enough for us to live there. So, we packed our things and moved to Roanoke, where we rented an apartment from my other brother-in-law's father-in-law. Things were going well until the money I was paying them for bills wasn't going into bills since all the bills were shared. Even though the house was broken into apartments, all the bills were connected as if it were still a house. I had quit my job for two weeks while I looked for something closer to where we lived because gas had become too expensive for me to commute. They told us the power had a disconnect notice and we needed to pay a certain amount of dollars so the power company wouldn't disconnect the lights. After learning they were lying about how much we needed to pay by confirming with the power company how much was owed and that there wasn't a disconnect notice, we packed up once again and moved into my dad's house. He was living in West Virginia; thus, we were living alone.

Abuse is something I have always sustained mentally, physically, psychologically, financially, and emotionally. Everywhere I have gone, there has been some form of abuse wielding power over my head. And everywhere I go, I am unwelcome to stay. Everywhere I go, I am not wanted and reminded of that. I am abandoned. I am thrown away. I am cast aside. I am not worthy to anyone. Do you know what that feels like? Do you know what it feels like to not be wanted, loved, or cherished by people who are either blood-related or related through marriage? The feelings are radically disheartening. I have been tossed away as trash plentiful enough throughout my life that I feel like trash. Maybe that's one reason I don't mind living in a messy house. I am just a piece of trash among the mix.

Dear Diary,

I now understand why dark souls are attracted to one another. At first, it didn't make sense. Those in the abyss seek out the light. Why would they search out the beacons of those floundering in chaos as they do? But it's simple, really. When they join their souls in this mortal coil, their chaos collides. From chaos, light is born. You are light, ready to explode.

Every person who has come into my life and left a truly remarkable memory was suffering as I did. They say that the more darkness that surrounds you, the brighter the light shines within you. For as long as I have been encased in darkness, I should be a show of a supernova star exploding in radiant colors to others, and I believe I am. It could be my words that people see and find comfort in to seek me out. It could be my want for joy and happiness breaking through the shadows that call out to others in the dark as well. It could be that they just see my light within and the struggle I have felt and kept that flame still burning brightly on my candle wick. I don't know what the drawing of others should be called, but I always attract those who are flailing, drowning, or needing a breath of air and somehow bring them to the surface.

My husband had never told me of the darkness he was in prior to meeting me. He drank and did drugs like many people our age did. He lived the life of the party, always chasing some form of high or release. And then he met me. At this time, I was just entering into the next dark phase of my life and the party stage of freedom as a twenty-one-year-old. I drank here and there to party, but I didn't do drugs, smoke weed or even smoke cigarettes. When he met me, I guess I sparked a change in his life, and he spent a couple of weeks getting his shit together. He stopped living the party life because I didn't live the party life. People had told me after we started dating that he had changed a lot after meeting me. I didn't understand what they meant until he told me much later in our relationship about how he was prior to meeting me.

There have been occasions when he has slipped back into that personality to cope with his own anxieties and depression, and I have pulled him out of it. That personality always brings skeletons with it and ghosts that aren't dead but just dead in his mind. His skeletons and ghosts have cut me deep throughout the years, making me feel the same unworthiness I have always felt. They've made me feel like my life with him was a façade. It was another moment of complex trauma etched into my psyche that has been remarkably hard to overcome. At times, I don't think I will ever overcome it. At times, I wonder if he ever

51

truly loves me or if he is here out of obligation. At times, he reminds me profoundly of my life before him, and it is exceedingly hard to overcome those feelings.

But to keep myself moving forward, I tell myself he wouldn't still be here or act in a caring manner if he didn't love me. I just hope those things are true and not something I am telling myself to later learn is just a ruse or a cruel joke in my mind. My mind is the killer of all things wonderful in my life. It kills my joy. It kills my happiness. It kills my love. It has tried to even kill me. But I fight it with every ounce of strength I have left to offer myself from over the years because there are people that need me here, and I cannot abandon them. So, I push it all down and tuck it away in a box that sometimes becomes so extraordinarily full it overflows into my life, which causes me to have to pick through the things I want to keep hidden and the things I want to completely erase. I would like to erase them all, but it only works one trauma at a time, and I have a trunk so exceptionally big I don't think I have the years left in life to completely empty that box of every single misery responsible for my depression. But I do take it one day at a time to try and get through it.

Dear Diary,

Have I always been too fucked up to know when someone cares about me and when they don't? It's always felt like a touch-and-go thing to me. I would have to say it was because of the bullying I faced throughout my formative years from home and kids my own age. I know peer pressure is one of the hardest things we face as adolescents. Most think peer pressure comes in the form of drugs and alcohol and rebellious behavior with partying and missing curfew, but it also comes in the form of behavior towards others your age.

I was bullied relentlessly, as I have said, and the bully had a friend that I had a crush on. Every person I had a crush on that they found out about in their circle of friends I was hounded over. But this one particular boy was the one that broke me in half, and I became submissive to their tactics. He once asked me out as a joke at lunch just to get his friends to laugh, the main one being the ringleader of the cruel joke. I felt like Martha "Dump Truck" from the Heathers movie. When he wasn't around his hoard of goons, he was a pretty decent guy. I got the balls once later on in school to ask if he wanted to date me, and he told me he wasn't seeing anyone and focusing on his schoolwork at the time. I later saw him walking down the hall with his arm thrown around another girl. Whether they were dating or just walking as friends I haven't a clue, but I assumed they were dating.

It was shattering to me. I was lied to. I was always lied to by people in my life; therefore, I was already used to it. But that day, I sat quietly on the bus waiting to be bussed over to another school for a class we took together, and he sat down next to me. Of course, music was the only solace I had, and I always had headphones on. I ignored him as he took his seat next to me with his loudmouth bully of a friend sitting behind us. He tapped me to get my attention, and I paused my music and looked over at him. He asked me a single question. "Are you mad at me?" And the only reply I could fathom was, "Why would I be mad at *you*?" And there was a quiet space between us and I'm certain I recognized in his eyes that he knew what it was but didn't say anything else. We rode in silence as I listened to my music.

The diary I had written the year prior, I was turning into a book. The class we took together was a type of creative writing class. I asked him if he would like to read what I had thus far because even if he bent under the peer pressure from his friends, I still liked him and considered him a friend. I never got my notebook back or the original story I had written.

Once he read it, he handed it over to his dad, who was a cop. His dad went to the teacher, and then the teacher came to me, asking me all the same questions I had heard before. And I was honest. My mother already knew about what I had written, and it was a story, and nothing was wrong at home, even though the last thing I told her was a lie. He had asked an adult for help for me.

I am notably used to asking for help and not receiving it being yelled at for it, or being told that it makes my parents look bad, that I stopped asking for help. I knew it wouldn't do any good considering my sister asked for help and she was left in the situation she was trying to get out of. I was angry he took the book to his dad. I was angry that I didn't get it back. I was angry I had to start the story over, and it lacked the depth it originally had. But now I see it differently. It was him caring for me. Sometimes, I think I let the bullying that I experienced drown out all the good that was in my life at the time. But the words people would say about me and talk about me made me feel inadequate to be his friend. Obsessive is a word that was used because I really liked him even though he didn't have the same feelings in our friendship. You can't just turn off a feeling just because it isn't reciprocated. I had one more class with him that he had friends in as well, but we didn't talk anymore and never got to be friends like we were in that one class.

I moved on from him as my crush, but he has always had a spot that I can never erase. Every person who leaves a mark on you throughout your life can never be truly forgotten. And even though my teenage mind was wrapped up in the aspect of dating, friendship was still important to me. It made me question if he ever did see me as a friend since once the class was over, we never really talked much again. Years later, we struck up a conversation online, I believe, on Myspace. We talked about things we had never shared in our formative years in high school, like my father being caught in the late 80s for growing a pot field. I invited him out with some friends to see a new movie showing that he said he was interested in seeing, but he never made it to the movies, and that was the last actual conversation we had. Years later, he would friend me on Facebook, and he would like the pictures I posted, which was surprising. The one I remember he liked in particular was the picture of my son when he was born, and we were in the hospital still.

He would later delete his Facebook and all social media accounts. I haven't seen nor heard from him in about ten years since his disappearance from social media. And yes, there are times I think about him and think about those particular years and what they were supposed to mean in the grand scheme of things. Sometimes, I have dreams of him where he tells me he did care for me even when I couldn't see it. Whether it was care for me as a friend or more, in the waking world, it didn't matter. Not until I remembered the notebook and the story and how I was wrapped up in being angry instead of recognizing that he was trying to get me help. People don't do that for others unless they have care for them unless they have empathy or sympathy for their situation. He didn't want me to hurt myself like the former diary had said I wanted to. I recognize that now. What do I do with it? I guess I use it to know that when people want to know how I am and say they want to help, they really do.

I have fooled myself into thinking for decidedly too long that people don't care about me because of my emotional abandonment, that I push away those who try to care for me. And the trust issues I have gained from those who have hurt me extremely over the years feed the anxiety and the fear of it all telling me no one really cares, but people have cared and more than just the one best friend who wanted to help me by getting an adult when I told her I was going to kill myself and telling he goodbye. There was another person in my life that had cared enough to not want me to hurt myself, and I just didn't see it at the time. But now I do, and I wish I could tell him thank you. I wish I could know how his mental health is as well. But fate works in mysterious ways, and I supposed our paths were only supposed to cross when they did countless years ago. At least now I can recognize it for what it was.

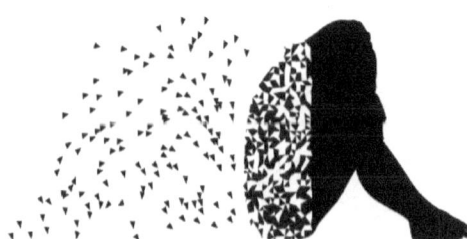

Dear Diary,

I grew up in a country music family, and I absolutely adore the Judds. It saddens me to know that her fight with severe depression, although made public (but unknown to my knowledge because I hadn't seen articles about it), wasn't spoken about in greater length. Robin Williams, Chester, and many, many celebrities who weren't given the recognition of drowning in the darkness while they were alive, and their deaths tip the scale for those of us who drown as well.

Mental health is greatly stigmatized, and mothers in the 80s and 90s refused to seek treatment because it meant they were crazy and couldn't raise their children properly. I experience depression from that stigma because even into the 2000s, my mother still felt that mental health instabilities were "taboo." The abuse I experienced due to the mental instabilities of my mother is still as fresh as the physical pain I felt when I was a child. Depression is almost like a crutch that helps me get through the pain, but it never ceases. I have always felt the need to tell people about the darkness and how they aren't alone.

However, even though it's a public topic and everyone wishes to raise awareness, we are still told it is taboo and stigmatized because they don't show depression in the news or media, and they hide it away from us, from those that don't experience it as if to protect them when we are the ones screaming for help. I don't think many understand when they post about "destigmatizing mental illness" because they only advocate that far. They don't demand to see more awareness where it matters most to society.

Society has blindly followed the media and magazines and news, latching onto many stigmas like how women should look or act. If the source of information in the modern day would talk more about depression and what happens from the experience, people would reach out for the help they need. They would reach out to people, and those people would know the signs and symptoms and reach out as well when they see loved ones struggling.

Needless to say, her death has affected me as well when she is me in the mirror. My depression won't help others fight the long fight until after I have died at the hands of it. My words mean nothing in the face of society because of fear of the taint that it could be on the masses of people who have healthy brain chemistry. "Shh, shh, she has mental illnesses," they whisper, but no one ever says, "How can I help?" They lend an ear to listen, or some just brush it off, but they don't take it to heart. It doesn't stop with a listening ear. It stops when people listen and proactively try to change that person.

I know everyone isn't a psychologist or psychiatrist or therapist, and it seems unfair to take burdens from other people. Why should you have to carry your own baggage along with someone else's? A lack of empathy has been the indoctrination of those who carry the power to change the world. They make us focus on things and then see everything else as negligence of ourselves. You're supposed to be fit, and if you aren't, you are unhealthy. You're supposed to be sane, and if you aren't, you need to be medicated to be like the rest of the sane world. Medication doesn't cure depression or other mental illnesses. It just alleviates the symptoms. You take away the medicine, and the brain chemistry is still fucked up.

Society views those who aren't medicated for their mental instabilities as negligent. "Why don't you take your medicine so you can be normal? You are just trying to make yourself be the way you are when there are fixes. It's attention-seeking. It's selfish. It's crying wolf." However, some of us are on our eighth prescription, the twentieth prescription, and it hasn't helped, or it has made it worse for us. Side effects of depression medications are the same side effects of depression. How can you "cure" something when the very thing touted as the fix-all remedy can increase the symptoms of our mental illness?

We don't want to talk to a stranger and have a stranger try to fix our problems through a magical talk paired with a pill that we must take every day for the rest of our lives just to function as a normal citizen. We don't want to lean into something that doesn't fix us. We want our flaws accepted for what they are and those in our lives that we love to be the shoulder to lean on and the crutch that helps us through our bad days. We don't want someone to hug us or just tell us that everything will be ok after we rip our hearts out and wear it on our sleeve for them. We want them to cry with us. We want them to come over and throw open our curtains and force us to look at the sunshine outside. We want them to make us a meal and sit down with us to ensure that we have eaten that day. We want them to tell us we smell and toss us a towel to shower while they prepare a spa day for us, where we paint each other's toenails or work on a project we enjoy. We want to be treated normally, but we also want them to let us know they care about us on a deeper level and are there for us at all costs.

It's that attachment to those around us that make or break us. We already feel alone and different. Even when we physically want to be left alone, it isn't healthy for us. We need to know that we aren't alone, even if we fight against it. Patting someone on their back wishing affirmations to us isn't what we really need and the reason why we don't reach out when it means the most to our existence. Those affirmations are just kind words. They don't feel heartfelt. We need to see the empathy. We need to feel the empathy. We want to feel alive while cobwebs hang in the corners of our souls, and the lightbulb that lit us from within has long burned out, ushering in the abyss we feel ourselves drowning in. We feel alive by connection with others. That connection with others is broken for us, and we need to be shown and not just told that it is there no matter what. That connection cannot be formed by a magic pill or a stranger that is a third person point of view in our story that has no real tie to us. Empathy and love are what help us get by day to day, and it means the most when it comes from someone that we adore. They are our lighthouse leading us to the shore, away from the dark pits we tumble through. That light is our salvation and our hope to make it another day, and it is meaningless unless we know it comes from the same place of emotion we hold within ourselves as well. People we love are our magic pill because we can't fix what's broken inside without them, especially when it was people who broke us by failing us in the beginning.

This does not negate the fact that there are those out there who abuse their mental illnesses because it gives them power over others. Not all people who are broken reach out for help but rather thrive in the ambiance of the insanity it brings with it. These people do not refuse medication because it worsens them or doesn't help, but they refuse it because they know it will make them better, and they no longer have an excuse for their toxic behavior. It isn't taboo to them or a stigma, but rather, the chaos of their chemical imbalance frees them from the consequences of their actions.

These aren't the people who promise to get help but become defeated along the journey and revert to the same self-destructive ways they reveled in. These are the people who openly abuse people and lean on their illness as the reason why and never try to adjust the situation to where they no longer harm people. They have no guilt or regret. They just have pleasure and borderline Munchausen that their attention-seeking behavior craves.

Dear Diary,

My parents were raised by a generation of parents who showed "tough love" or apathy when it came to their kids. I remember once my mom told me the story of how she ran her hand through a window on a door, and after coming to from passing out, her mother showed no concern for it except for chastising her siblings for not telling her about the accident. I could remember the same type of concern while growing up.

I remember I touched the top of a kerosene heater because my parents didn't have the safety guard on it. We were running around the house playing tag, and I stopped to take a breather and leaned on it (It was a flat-top one). I was burned badly and probably needed to go to the hospital for first- or second-degree burns. My mom rubbed some lotion that had some aloe vera in it on the burn, then wrapped it in ice. I woke up in the middle of the night screaming because the ice had melted and it was burning again. I was in pain for several days, but I wasn't taken to the doctor to have it looked at. I don't remember where my dad was because it happened in his living room, which was blocked off by a wall from my mother's, and there was a doorway to her room and a half wall to the dining room behind his. So, I was running from the doorway through the kitchen into the dining room, past the half wall into his living room and repeating it.

I remember my brother's first wife was there that night and was the one who kept putting ice on my hand. I was watching Are You Afraid of the Dark on Nickelodeon, and the episode was about the kid who drowned when they let the dam loose. I do know I was around the same age then that I was when my parents started seeing a pain management doctor. Ergo, this could have been when my dad first started selling pills.

I also remember when we would go swimming in our kiddie pool, we had a door that we used to get in and out so we wouldn't get the pool dirty. It was one of those old, thick, heavy metal doors that went on houses. My sister hadn't had the chance to spray it down with water to make sure it wasn't too hot for us when I slipped and fell on it. I burned a huge red spot on my thigh. The burn was about 6 inches in diameter across my thigh. I'm pretty sure she got in trouble for it, even though it wasn't really her fault. It was an accident. I have a picture of us where she is spraying the door down with the water hose while we are playing in the pool. She did it quite often while we were in the pool to make sure I didn't get burned again. The burn was bad, and it hurt to walk. Mom took me with her to Food Lion to go shopping, and I laid on the bottom of the buggy's grate, where you can put your sodas or whatever, holding a towel with ice against it.

Another time I should have been taken to the hospital or a doctor was when I got severe sun poisoning. I was outside swimming in the pool all day long. I remember when the sun went down, the sunburn started hurting like normal. My mom was asleep on the couch while my sister had been watching me. I know the burn got so intense that night that I woke up screaming in pain, and she would pour ice-cold water on my back to help soothe the burn. I was blistered from my neck down to my mid-back and down my arms to my elbows. I couldn't move for days and had to sleep on my stomach in the living room while lotion with aloe vera was applied to the burn.

Since that sunburn, I have taken extra precautions to prevent burns like that again. I have had blister sunburns since then, but not as bad until I was about 22 years old and went strawberry picking. I went to the doctor, and he asked me several times if I was sure it was a sunburn and not a chemical burn because the burn was pretty bad. It wasn't nearly as bad as it had been when I was a kid.

Dear Diary,

I miss the child who saw the world through a painted lens of rose-colored joy. Throughout all the darkness and woes and despair, she had stars in her eyes and dreams within her grasp. However, her roots were never watered. Nothing special had ever come from those who lived in this family. Unless it was achieved through illegal or solicited activities, grandness was a wishful thought. I dreamed of greatness for myself like every wistful child does. But that greatness was not nurtured.

Yeah, sure. My mother pushed me to graduate school. My mother like my aspirations of college to become a doctor or a lawyer. But it wasn't until my adulthood, before she started to see that I had a creative drive to myself. I loved art. I loved writing. I loved music. I loved multitudes of creative things that I was never nurtured in. She had seen my sketches and would say how well they were drawn but would not pay for art lessons. I loved music, but she wouldn't pay for guitar lessons. I had to teach myself everything I knew about my creative side. My father played guitar very well but would not sit down to teach me anything, although he had taught my brothers. The lack of care for my interests led to those interests slowly dying throughout the years.

I miss the little girl who used to grow wildflowers in her soul. They were such vibrant colors that illuminated any room she would grace with her presence. That little girl was so full of hope and so full of life. She saw beauty in chaos as she was taught from chaos, life had sprung. She dreamed in technicolor and believed in faith. I miss the little girl I used to be a long time ago before grey skies moved in and swallowed me whole, trapping me in an abyss that even God couldn't control. I was moving mountains with aspirations, and those slowly wilted and withered like an unkempt garden in the summer's heat. And now, I water dead flowers in my soul, hoping that the water can rejuvenate what was stolen from me as a child. I reach out to people through words, hoping they can see the chance of beauty that lies deep in the weeds of what once thrived as a fairytale kingdom.

Pieces of my truth blow in the wind, landing in jigsaw puzzles of ruins from the words that I inked into the walls of my mind. My soul has been on fire for so long that I fear it will destroy the other parts of me that I kept locked away safe. Now, all that's left of a soul that burned beautiful and bright are ashes in a field from a burning house locked in my memory. I felt as if I kept that part of me alive and that the parts of me that begged for reprieve would suffer endlessly. So, I set fire to the walls of my prison and burned them to the ground, killing both my monsters and a part of myself I never thought I would regain. I walked the halls with gasoline and matches. Embers and ash rain from the sky of what used to be my fairytale kingdom. I had let the weeds overgrow the foundation, and for every weed that caught fire once I started the blaze, a part of myself was released into awareness. It was as if a volcano exploded, and the raining bits of internal rage were released into the air but cooled too rapidly. Monsoons and earthquakes couldn't rid the evidence left behind from my fire.

What I didn't know is that wildfires that burn hot and out of control have a purpose in nature. Once the destruction has ceased and the fires and smoke have been cleared, new life begins to grow from the rubbles of chaos that lit the match. What I thought I had destroyed within me was beginning to regrow with beautiful new colors. I had not killed the part of me I would never get back. I had rebirthed it instead into another creature entirely. And as I grew, the ashes that had been left behind were absorbed into the plant's nutrients and made available to bear witness to the memories I had long abandoned and thought I had erased and killed. I could now see them for what they were. I could understand everything, and the whys and hows were answered for me. My kingdom was being restored, but it wasn't. I wasn't rebuilding the same castle all over again. I was building a new and improved castle where I didn't feel the need to be saved. I felt free instead.

The little girl inside of me is begging to be set free to speak but the only words she ever feared were sit down, shut up, and act like you're not here. That little girl has been silenced for so long with excuses and fear that even as I speak of my past, I am reminded that it's supposed to be a secret. It's not supposed to be spoken out loud. It's not supposed to be told. It's not supposed to be available to the public eye. It's supposed to be hidden, buried, and pushed down. It's supposed to be forgotten as if it had never happened. I fear with each word spoken that I will be in trouble. I fear with each word spoken there will be consequences. I fear that with each word spoken, I will feel the lashing of my mother's hand across my face, shattering my little girl. So, I have kept that little girl locked away from the world, locked in silence, suspended in an eternal slumber, withholding the truth of our existence. I tried to kill the little girl inside of me in order to eradicate everything she had ever experienced, hoping it would die with her. However, that little girl has banged on that locked door with fear from being alone and solitary for so long that my soul bleeds from her torn and fractured hands as I grow with a piece of myself missing. That little girl is the puzzle piece I need to make myself whole, and I have repressed her for so long. I have tried to erase her for countless numbers of years, but I am afraid of what damnation she brings along with her chaos and wonderment.

Every time the little girl has pounded on the door to be set free, I have never felt safe enough to do so other than telling people extremely close to me. One reason was that someone would tell me that what I experienced was trivial. That it didn't surmount to enough to be considered abuse. That they experienced far worse than me, so what's the big deal. That I was experiencing discipline and character building, and I was making a big deal out of nothing. So, I have kept her quiet with comforting things. I have satiated her with food when she would call out, starving for affection. I have sung her lullabies in hopes she would sleep in wonderland and not have to witness the reality at hand. I have rocked her to sleep when her cries were too loud to drown out. I have played her music to soothe her anxiety and sensory overload that has led to tantrums or miserable depression. I have watched movies and television shows with her to entertain her. I have read her books to show her worlds upon worlds while locked away from the rest of the actual world. When she would beg for the light of day, I would assure her that the sun was rising soon and she would be free from the darkness I kept her in. That darkness built up like a raging storm building on the shores of the beach and eventually turned into a hurricane. When she drowns in the rising waters, I drown alongside her. Even though she is locked away, she experiences nothing without me by her side, assuring her that everything will be fine and that everything will be ok but for today, she needed to stay quiet and hidden because it was not safe for her.

She isn't allowed to answer the door when knocks come to it for unsuspected visitors to upset her. She isn't allowed to look through the windows to witness the world burning down around her. She is kept safe and sound in her room. It is not safe for her out in the world until I can hold her in my arms and cover her with a blanket while walking her through the renewed gardens that have been grown from pure destruction. She doesn't need to see what it took for me to get her out of the dark. She just needs to be able to see what I have given her in return as the warmth of the sun kisses her skin.

Dear Diary,

It always feels like no one wants to keep my kids because they don't want them around. I know they feel the same as I feel regarding them as well. They have asked me questions before about it. I remember those feelings all too well as a child. Since I was a bedwetter, I wasn't welcome to stay at many places. I remember once I spent a weekend for the first time at my grandparents' house, and I was chastised and ridiculed every morning by my grandmother for wetting the bed. She was pissed off that she had to wash the bedding. It was the first and last time I ever spent the night there.

I remember it would irritate my siblings if I stayed and wet the bed. In particular, my sister would tell me it embarrassed her and angered her that I wet the bed, and what nights I did spend at her house, I was made to sleep on the floor where I wouldn't ruin anything of hers. When she took me on vacation with her, she was angry every morning that I wet the sheets on the couch I was sleeping on. It wasn't until she had children of her own that wet the bed long into childhood and their teenage years that she felt the sympathy for me that I needed then.

Flash forward to when my mother passed. I was staying with my brother. He even gave me my own room in his house. When he and his wife split up, he left. One of the reasons I was tremendously eager to stay with him was because we had never had time to get close my entire life, and when the chance presented, it was yanked away as soon as it fell in my lap. A lot of drama later, and it was clear that he wasn't happy with me living in the house anymore. His wife moved out, and there was no one there anymore. Consequently, I bounced from couch to couch between my sister, my other brother, and my dad's house.

I was welcome to stay at my dad's house, but we didn't get along at all and I still held feelings towards him about the way he treated me living there before. I had already had issues with my other brother staying there with my mother, and my sister made it painstakingly clear she didn't want me living with her. So, not only was I abandoned by my mother upon her death, but it felt like everyone in the family abandoned me. To stay places, I had to make myself worthy of being there, and I was often made to feel unworthy. It didn't matter what I did. I was a burden.

My kids always ask to spend the night at different family members' houses. I have often made plans with some of them that fell through quite often enough that when they ask to get the kids, I no longer tell them they might be spending the weekend there because I don't want them to feel unwanted when those plans fall through for them to stay. For the longest time, the only surviving grandparent they had left didn't want to keep them. Even when both of their grandparents on their father's side were alive, they acted as if they didn't want to keep them just because of me.

Now, I run into a different issue with their grandpa. There have been a couple of times I have asked his girlfriend if they wanted to get the kids, and she's told me no, while he has told me to bring them. Undoubtedly, she doesn't want them around. She doesn't like me either. Another issue I run into is he still gets the grandkids of his ex-girlfriend, and they give my kids lice, which takes what seems like forever to get rid of. They miss school. It's more of a nuisance than anything, and it is frustratingly a catch-22. He's the only person that is willing to keep them but also, I have to treat their heads for lice every time they stay. It's time-consuming. It's costly.

I am just tired. I am tired of feeling what I feel because of how I was raised, and I am tired that my kids seem to feel the same way as well. I shower them with all the love and affection I can fathom to the surface, but it's not always enough to just have one person consistently show and tell them they are wanted and loved. Not to mention, it becomes quite tiring not ever having a break to myself. It's 24/7 mom duty.

I recently started taking Xanax to control my anxiety because it has been uncontrollable and raging for about a year. Our car broke down over the summer; therefore, I was literally stuck in the house for nearly three months without a way to go anywhere and with them the entire time, day and night. No one offered to get them and keep them. No one bothered to see if I needed a break. No one ever wonders how I function mental health wise over things. I became extremely stressed out over the summer, and toward the end, I started having serious body pain and issues. It wasn't until I tried some antianxiety medication that everything subsided, and I knew it was my anxiety at its breaking point. I didn't want a prescription for it but needed it because the anxiety and stress were starting to present themselves physically. It felt like I had a broken neck, and there was this intense pressure band from the nape of my neck that wrapped my entire head and made my face numb. At one point, I thought I was having a stroke, which made the anxiety worse. It descended through my torso and made my chest hurt for days. My esophagus felt like it was on fire, and with every breath and bite of food or drink of drink I took felt like red-hot needles were sliding down my throat. I also felt the sensation of something consistently stuck in my throat. My entire body hurt. It caused me to gain weight that I had worked exceedingly hard to lose, which triggered me more. Xanax was the only thing that alleviated the pain.

I subconsciously was that child stuck inside the house, not allowed to go anywhere. I was imprisoned in my own home. And it seemed as if no one cared, just like when we had to live in a motel for a few months because our power was shut off and we didn't have the money to catch it up. I was stuck with three kids, all of them much younger than now, and no one bothered to offer to keep them but one time. It always feels like I am an afterthought, that no one truly cares how I mentally and emotionally process things. And it also makes me feel like my children are an afterthought to the same people who are their actual blood family. I am simply married into the family, but they are blood-related, and it feels as cold as my own family does at times.

Getting a babysitter these days is nearly impossible, not to mention the trust issues I have with people and my kids as it is, considering family has been the ones that lost my child. Date night is a relatively new thing for my husband and me due to the lack of people to keep our kids. We get a date night maybe once or twice a year if we are lucky, and I make sure it's around our wedding anniversary. Even the day we got married, which was post having a child, his parents would only keep our oldest overnight and were demanding our return early the next morning. Therefore, we never had an actual honeymoon. It was just a night in a hotel room after we had dinner with his brother and sister-in-law.

People don't recognize that all these things, when compounded, cause complex PTSD. Abandonment issues, trust issues, feelings of being unwanted, unloved, unworthy, and a burden. Add to that crippling anxiety, depression, bipolar, and child abuse in many different forms, and you have one fucked up mind that feels broken all the time. And when those feelings are triggered, it is immensely hard not to lash out or be irritable and angry and all types of mixed emotions. At times, it's unbearable to function like a normal adult except to put on a charade and placate a persona and wear a happy face just so your kids don't see it, but they do. My oldest does, and I hate that she sees it. I hate that she sees the side of me that I try to suppress and keep caged because I don't want it to affect how I raise them. But it slips out occasionally, and her empathetic nature is nurturing when it does, but she shouldn't have to be the one to nurture me. It should be me nurturing her and her siblings. And they shouldn't have to witness when my rage and anger and irritability flare because I have been triggered either. But one thing I do that was never done for me is apologize for it and explain to them the whys and how I am working to not do it even though it doesn't happen that often in their presence. But I am trying, and I suppose that counts. I just hate being terribly broken. And I hate that they see it and know it.

Dear Diary,

Depression is the gift that keeps on giving. There are countless times that I have apologized in my head for things I shouldn't even think. The "I'm sorrys" have always built from the anxiety of not feeling worthy or good enough. I have always felt like a fuck up even though I show perfectionism on the outside. I feel like I only mess things up, and I can't do anything right. I feel like a failure at numerous things. These feelings make me feel like a burden, a waste of space, a waste of time. People can tell me how I mean so much to them, but it just falls into an empty hole within me that I keep for all positive comments to be eaten away by shadows of depression.

It doesn't help that there have been plenty of others who lay their own issues and their own faults on me, and I take the blame for everything horrible that goes wrong. But I take it because I was built for it. It's all I heard growing up that this is my fault and that is my fault. Naturally, even when the blame falls on others, I take it as my own. My own personal image of myself has been shards of a mirror tossed at me with pictures glued to the glass to show me how others feel and see me instead of allowing me to see me for me.

My perception of myself has always been askew. No one had ever told me I was beautiful inside and out. I was told I had a beautiful soul. A beautiful soul is what you tell ugly people to make them feel better. I had always been overweight and obese. Therefore, I already knew I was ugly, and it just added gasoline to the fire whenever I heard those words. I wanted someone to see the beauty that was outside as well as what they said I had on the inside. I wanted to be told I was beautiful no matter what my dress size was. No one ever did. Instead, I was criticized for it relentlessly. My body dysmorphia had grown so bad there were times that the thought crossed my mind to just pick up a knife and slice the fat from my body. There are times I still think of doing those things. They're intrusive thoughts, and I would never really do it, but the thought has occurred to me. And I went many years without hearing that I was attractive that now when I hear it, I think it's just because they think it's what I want to hear and don't really mean it.

Dear Diary,

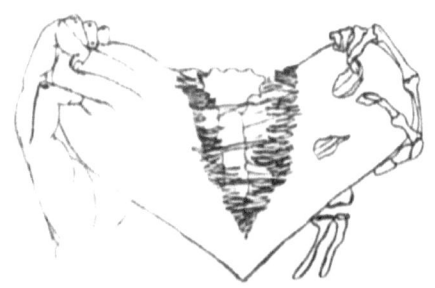

I have never asked to be saved. I have never reached out to people to allow them into my circle of trust. I am vulnerable there. I don't know what they think of me. I don't know if they believe me. I don't know if they think what happened was okay or not. I don't want to share the dark crevices of my mind with people because I don't feel as if they could relate to me or that they would judge me. The few times I have reached out to people with problems, they were dismissed, swept under the rug, briefly recognized, and moved on from.

My fragility is precious to me. I have been fragile since a child. I live in a fragile world in a fragile state of being where just a tiny bit of movement would shatter the glass tight rope that I walk across. I am socially inept due to my crippling social anxiety from trying to assimilate into the normal population as an abnormal person that didn't fit society's standards. "Poor you, your mother called you fat. People are dying in a war right now. Their issues are more important." "Poor you, your parents abused you. At least you had parents because there are kids growing up without them that would have loved the experience." "You don't have scars, so it couldn't

81

have been that bad of abuse." "You're just one of the emo kids that cry woe is me and use mental illness as a trending thing." "Everyone has their own problems and own skeletons in the closet. Deal with it like they do." "I would have made fun of you too. Look how big you are."

I run these things over in my mind because of how often I was reminded I was worthless. I fear rejection, and sharing that fear leads to worry and obsessive thinking about whether you rejected me behind my back while being nice to my face. This has been my experience for years, and nothing will ever change that from immediately being the first thing I think of when I tell someone something about myself. That and plus the fear of them telling others and then a group of people mocking me behind my back.

Dear Diary,

I was not a great friend when I was in school, and there are many things I regret about my relationship with my former best friend. One of those things is nearly killing her, whether she realizes it now or not. My mom bought me diet pills to take. In the beginning, I was like sure! I'd love to take them and lose this weight. I had heard my entire life I was fat and those magic pills would make me skinny and normal like everyone else.

She bought me all kinds of different diet pills, and what was once an encouragement to take them soon became a demand. "Did you take your diet pills?" "Don't forget your diet pills." "Here, take this. It's a diet pill." The diet pills weren't working, and she just bought more and more, thinking I wasn't taking them. One brand she bought me was labeled as "Mini thins." This brand has since been banned in the country due to it having epinephrine in it, and people were using it to get high. It was speed in a bottle. If I took the pills, I would need to feel like I had to move more, and the weight would come off. I never admitted to how they made me feel anxious or made my heart beat fast. I couldn't sleep right after taking them. But they were the miracle pill. My sister had lost weight on them therefore I could too!

I didn't understand how dangerous those pills were. I didn't understand how dangerous any diet pill really was until I started having stomach problems. But I took those pills to school with me, and I talked about those pills with my best friend, who had her own body image issues. She was beautiful and slim already, so when she asked for some to take, I didn't understand why she would want them. I gave her a few of them. The next day, she was tweaking. She asked me if she was supposed to take all of them in one day, and I very passionately told her no. She was experiencing the same feelings I had been while taking them, but much worse. I had given her four pills. I took one a day. The bottle instructed up to two a day. She doubled the dose. I was frightened. I could get in trouble for giving those to her.

We weren't supposed to have medication on us. It had to be through the nurse at school. Well, they wouldn't give out medication without a prescription. These pills were diet pills you bought at the convenience store. They wouldn't allow that. Not only did I bring meds to school, but I also gave those meds to another student. That's breaking the law, and I could get expelled for that, even though it was just a diet pill. Lastly, I didn't even know it at the time, but those pills were dangerous. I knew she could have been hurt badly after I realized she had taken all those pills. I could have killed her. It would have been my fault. I would have lived with that guilt, knowing that my mother's obsession with her fat daughter caused her daughter to think it was okay to hand out those same pills to her friends because she didn't know they were dangerous. She asked for more pills that same day she said they made her feel weird. I told her no.

I have never claimed to be perfect. I know I am the furthest away from perfect as they get. I would be in my twenties before I ever tried recreational drugs, but I did try them. Not all of them. I wasn't out there hitting a crack pipe or smoking methamphetamines. I did try cocaine, though. The way cocaine made me feel was the same way those diet pills made me feel. As a teenager, we are unaware of the dangers of pills. I still didn't even know my dad had a drug problem at this time. I didn't know that if I had conceded to my friend asking for more pills and given her some, I could have ended up turning her into an addict. It's one of the guilts I now live with, whether it affected her on the same level as it did me. But I did know that by telling her no, I wasn't going to be responsible if she took those pills all at once again and died.

Dear Diary,

I'm looking into a pool of despair. A child lost in innocence. The need to run but also the need to stay. The need to endure to make those happy, which causes our unhappiness. The need to bend over backwards for approval. Approval that is not recognized or nonexistent. A child lost in the depths of woes. A family breached and incapable of pulling back together. A child that just wants to be happy. Wants their parents to be happy. And, in consequence, will solicit to their undying requests. Ones that could mean life or death. And the child succumbs to these pleas. The thirst for love and appreciation fuels their every whim. But the child remains lost as the last breath is taken. And nothing was ever done to help, only to destroy. Who can help the child now when they failed to love and instead strove to please?

My mother had been sick my entire life with cardiovascular disease. At the age of thirteen, my mother had open heart surgery, and from that point on, I was her caretaker. I assumed any duties in the house that she couldn't complete. I cooked dinner for everyone. I made sure she took her pills. I essentially became the mother. It's hard for a child to become the head of the house even when the title isn't officially bestowed on them. But I was still reminded all the time that I was lazy. I was reminded that I had duties to the house even when I was an adult. It was my job to make sure everyone ate because my mother was always sleeping.

When my mother died, I was emotionally distraught and frayed. I was 20 and still living with her and under her thumb of rule. I was an adult still being bossed around as if I were a child. I had no concept of a relationship other than the mother-daughter dynamic. I felt unwanted by my family. Shortly after moving in with my brother, he moved out, and I was there with his wife and kids. There isn't a strong bond between us because my mother never allowed me to really visit family even though they literally lived next door. I wasn't allowed to leave the house except for when I went to my sister's house. I wasn't allowed to live there either, nor did I feel comfortable living with my other brother after my mother and I had left his house to live with my father again a few days before her death. I felt alone, and when the time came for me to leave my brother's house, the only option I really had was my father's house.

I honestly blamed myself for my mother's death for years. After she had suffered her stroke, she was in my care mostly. People helped when we lived with my brother, but it was mostly my responsibility when I was there to care for her. The only times I really wasn't there were when I was in school or when I spent a week at my sister's house sick. When we moved back in with my dad, I had gone to the movies with a friend and got home right around midnight. I put my mother to bed and slept on the couch so I could help her in the middle of the night if she needed it. About an hour or two into sleep, I awoke to her vomiting and running a fever in her sleep. She hadn't woken up, so I let her be, cleaned the mess, and tried to get some more sleep since I was running on empty of energy. I woke up several times, checking her breathing and her fever. Her fever had broken but she was making an unusual sound with her breathing, but a sound she had made before. When I would shake her, she wouldn't wake up but that was also normal for her as well. I checked to make sure she was propped right in bed before falling back asleep. I awoke again to check on her, and that time, her breathing was too strange to ignore. She wasn't breathing the right number of breaths per minute. I ran to get the phone to dial 911 and told my father what was happening. After dialing 911, I called both of my brothers to come up there immediately. Right as the ambulance pulled into the driveway, she stopped breathing in my one brother's arms, and he had started CPR. They didn't have a defibrillator in their ambulance. They announced her DOA at the hospital.

I play that night and morning over and over in my head. Did I do everything right? Should I have called

911 sooner? Varying different scenarios ran through my head, and I felt ashamed and guilty. I could have probably saved her life had I called sooner. I was a baby, though. I had no life experience. I had no medical training. I had nightmares for weeks after of me physically murdering her in my dreams because I blamed myself greatly for her death. I got a job at a bar shortly after and began to drink. They didn't care if you worked the floor and drank behind the bar while on the clock. I took a shot here and there but didn't drink in excess because I had to drive home. Drinking made me happy. I was never really a woe-is-me person when I drank, other than one time when I was going through a really hard time accepting the fact that my ex-boyfriend was ghosting me.

Why is this important? I didn't start processing her death and my life living with my parents until after my father had died. My father passed away several years ago from alcohol and drug abuse, killing his liver. We had to pull him off life support, and it took a good hour or two for him to pass as he struggled to breathe. I had nightmares of him as well, dying over and over. Each time he would flat line, he would take in a breath, and it would start all over again. I went through a severe depression from his death and the culmination of my life up until then.

I had barely spoken with my father in the past years up to his death since he lived in West Virginia, and I hardly ever kept a phone. When he was in the last time, he was drinking, and I was the one that was buying it for him when he asked me to. He wasn't allowed to drink at my brother's house. I felt to blame once again for giving in to a parent who asked me to buy them something. He was an adult and could make his own decisions. We didn't know his liver had gone back to bad shape after he reversed it the first time.

It would be the following year after his death when I was forced into therapy and onto medication, that I began to realize the abuse I had suffered at my parents' hands was actual abuse. Before therapy began, I had started to come to the realization that I had suffered abuse. I had PTSD from it. My sister once told me that I didn't experience anything worth having PTSD from our parents because she didn't have PTSD from her abuse. My sister escaped the abuse at the age of 16 when she emancipated herself. The difference between us was my parents flat out told me they wouldn't let me leave like her. They would fight it if I tried to leave. I had no job experience because I wasn't allowed to work. I had no social experience because I wasn't allowed to do ANYTHING. I had no relationships outside of my hours at school.

Dear Diary,

I always wonder if my children know how much I love them. Really, really know how much I love them. Do I hug them enough? Do I spend enough time with them during the day? Do I tell them how important they are enough? Do I tell them how beautiful they are enough? Do I shine enough light on their lives that they won't grow up as miserable as I did? Will the child inside of them be able to shine in the future as bright as the sun? Or have I failed them? Do they not think any of this about me?

With all the hatred in the world, I fear how it will stunt their empathy and compassion. I fear it will lead to them pushing the world away instead of embracing it headstrong and full of wonder. I fear this world will swallow them whole, and if it does, that they will feel there is nowhere or no one to turn to for help because I failed them. My children are my whole world, and I know every mother says that, but it is the only world I live in. I stay home with them. I nurture them. I try every which way to let them know that I love them. But I still fear that they don't really know. Am I too harsh with punishments when they don't do their chores? Are my words too harsh whenever I am frustrated?

Until I was around 11-12 years old, my sister raised me. It was my sister that woke me to get me ready for school. It was my sister that walked me to the bus stop. It was my sister that walked me home from the bus stop. It was my sister who showed me compassion when my mother would punish me for wetting the bed. My mother grounded me to a corner once for the entire day for wetting the bed. When she left to go to the store for the day, my sister let me out of the corner until the headlights appeared through our sliding glass doors, and she quickly ushered me back to the chair I had been punished to. It was my sister that would play with me and spend time with me. It was my sister that would sit in my room and watch movies with me. My sister cared for me through the night whenever I would get a bad sunburn and cry from pain.

And then my sister grew up. She no longer wished to do the things with her little sister that she once did. She wanted space. She wanted privacy, and I was the annoying little sister who was a tag-along that she "had" to bring places. She wanted to hang out with people her own age. She wanted to have boyfriends. She wanted time away from me. The only person who ever did things with me was no longer there for me while under the same roof.

And then my sister left me to escape her own abuse. I was left completely alone, not allowed to leave the house. Not allowed to socialize with the family that lived around. I wasn't allowed to do anything but clean and sit in my room. My mother often slept. My father had his own space that most would attribute to a man cave modernly where he would drink beer all day. My only friends were characters in books or on TV, and I ravaged books and movies to escape my own reality. We never had family time. We never had family vacations, and I have made sure to make that a staple with my kids. We always take them everywhere with us.

But I still wonder if they know that everything we do for them is because we love them. While having lunch one day with my oldest and her friends at school, she asked her friends if they had strict parents. I waited for her to explain what strict parents were because we were very lax with everything, with the exception of her not being allowed to have a phone because she didn't follow the rules about social media. When she explained, she told them she had chores they had to do. Her little friend immediately piped up and said she had chores, and it's good to do chores to help your mom out around the house. A sigh of relief spread throughout me hearing both of their responses during the conversation. I did have strict parents. I lived the life of a fairytale princess waiting to be saved by her Prince Charming. My Prince Charming drove a black chariot and wielded a scythe, but no less, I was saved.

I always tell people, had my mom not died, that I have no clue where I would be in life. The main reason I didn't go off to college was because of her health. I was worried that what adult time I could spend with her would be wasted while I was hours away from her. I was always in a constant state of anxiety when it came to my mother because I loved my mother and still love my mother, even accepting the abuse I withstood. That abuse molded me as a mother, and I don't even like to discipline my children because it feels like child abuse if I do. I don't know what is ok and what is not. Is popping them on the butt too much? And when they cry when they are in trouble, it breaks my heart because I feel their tears because I experienced their tears growing up.

A lot of times, I catch myself in an angry mood swing and must be careful what I say so I don't say something that would traumatize their brains. There are times that I don't know if what I said is ok or not. It's hard raising children after being raised by abusive parents when it comes to discipline, and I am always afraid that the discipline I show comes off as too harsh of a punishment. So, when I yell at them to clean and take their things from them, I never follow through with the punishment nor make them clean because I know what it was like for me. I also know they need to learn discipline; hence, it's a catch-22 for it all. I can only hope that, moving forward, my children really know I love them. So, I tell them every day. I try not to let my own mental health affect my raising them, but it is hard. But I tell them I love them every single day. I hug them every single day. I shower them with love every single day. Or at least I think I do? I hope I do... because I don't want to cause my children to be as dysfunctional in relationships as I am or have to think about what is right and what is wrong when it comes to those relationships and structure. I want them to know what love is so they don't experience abuse at the hands of the wrong person.

I try to express my joy and appreciation whenever they give me gifts whether it is crafted art or present from the store. I recall one Christmas as a teenager, I had been given money to buy my mother a gift, and she had pointed out some rings she really liked. When I went to get the rings, they only had one of them left, and I grabbed it since it was the same stone. It was a heart-shaped alexandrite gold ring. When my mother opened it on Christmas Eve during our family get-together, her face scrunched, and she huffed at me. "This isn't the one I wanted," she said and set the gift aside. I left the room and went to the bathroom to cry because it really hurt my feelings that she didn't like the expensive present I had gotten her. Family members said something to her before coming to check on me after I tried to hide my red-speckled, puffy face by splashing cold water on it. She apologized to me and thanked me for the gift, but those words remain burned into me. So, whenever my children shower me with gifts or artwork or crafted cards, I smile and truly feel the love of the gift they are giving me. I thank them and tell them I love it. I smile big for them so they will never feel as if they let me down over a gift that is supposed to be a reflection of the love they have for me.

But I still wonder every single day, do my children know I love them? Because with my mother, I never really did.

Dear Diary,

Most people don't know what parentification is or what it means. Parentification is where the child is the parent when the parent lacks in the department or where they treat the child as an adult, leaning on them for personal venting. Much of what I experienced growing up was through parentification, like taking care of my mother or cleaning the whole house because they didn't, and it was my job to do it. The instance of my mother lashing out about my depression instead of helping me cope with it was parentification. My sister, as well with her taking care of me until she moved out.

Parentification leads to many of the issues I have, such as insecure attachments in relationships, trust, and abandonment. Most often, I find it hard to put my feelings into words unless it is through writing and poetry. I feel like I had a lost childhood as well as struggle with self-blame and guilt a lot over what happened. It causes depression, stress, and anxiety, as well as stomachaches and headaches, much of which I dealt with growing up.

Parentification is considered abuse in today's psychological standards. Parents who do this usually have substance abuse issues, mental health issues, or even chronic health problems, all of which were in my household. Being a caretaker for my mother from her heart issues and picking up all the duties she forewent was part of parentification. Along with what is said negatively to children, the lack of affirmations, praise, and positive feedback, along with other things that go along with it, causes trauma. It's the feeling of not feeling welcome in the world, which is a deep root in my psyche. I have never felt wanted or loved.

In cases of the parent treating the child as an adult to lean on and vent, I am not sure of what my siblings know about my mother in the few years leading up to her death. The persona my parents put on was a "deep in love" one. However, I was a junior in high school when she asked me if it would bother me to change schools and go to a different school my senior year. I honestly didn't care. It would have gotten me away from the bullying and abuse I sustained during school hours. She had plans of leaving my father and moving in with her dad and stepmother. We talked about it for a couple of weeks, and I never knew what the deciding factor was of her not going through with it. I remember she had called an ex-lover of hers, and after she realized he wouldn't leave his wife for her, she changed our phone number so his wife wouldn't call to speak to my dad.

Once, my mother was scheduled for a stent catheterization for her heart problems. They told her to take her main medication before going into the hospital. She accidentally took the wrong pill for her blood pressure medicine and took a sleeping pill by mistake. By the time she was being prepped for surgery, she couldn't stay awake, and they had no idea what was wrong. She ended up in the emergency room and then was admitted to the hospital. The levels of pain pills and barbiturates in her system were normal, so she hadn't taken too much pain medication or anxiety medication. It would be later when I became the person who oversaw her daily medications, that I realized her amitriptyline looked just like her blood pressure medication.

Had it not been for me telling her doctor that she hadn't overdosed on medication like the hospital had said (they said they gave her Narcan, and she woke up when she didn't wake up at all after the Narcan), she would have lost her pain medication prescription. I also told him that I was not in charge of her medications. A similar event happened when she had pneumonia when I was in college, and once again, I had to explain to her doctor that she had not overdosed on pain medicine and had pneumonia that caused low oxygen levels and an inability to wake her.

When she was in the hospital over the wrong medication, it was when the county fair was in town. My bother and his family were going to the fair and said I could come with them too. So, I went. My mother was stable. She was sleeping. She was fine. I could release my anxiety over the last two days and blow some steam off having fun. My mother didn't see it that way. She shamed me for going out and having fun. I even said my brother and everyone went, but I was the only one who she found it offensive to have fun while she was in the hospital.

When I was seventeen, I had my gallbladder removed. I was out of school for more than a week, recovering from the surgery. I was in constant pain and had pain pills that literally knocked me out. I slept through most of the days, just waking up long enough to snack on something and drink something or go to the bathroom. I was woken up by my sister one morning. She was there to drop the kids off, and mom wouldn't wake up, so she was making me watch the kids. I told her I couldn't stay awake from the pain medication and I was in too much pain to watch them. They were only like three or four-years-old maybe younger, so they were a lot to handle. She didn't care. She left them anyway. So, I was forced to get up and spent nearly the entire day watching the kids. I can't remember if my mom woke up or my sister returned from her appointment, which let me off the hook of watching them. I was in so much pain by the time I was able to take my pain medicine because I couldn't take it while watching them, or I would have fallen asleep. She could have taken the kids with her to the appointment she was going to. She had a friend driving her. He could have watched them while she went in.

There were quite a few times I was forced to watch her kids without my consent or want to watch them. She would check me out of school without asking our mom, or she would tell me I was spending the weekend with her just to find out I was her non-paid babysitter. It got to the point where when I stayed on the weekends when the kids woke up, I didn't get up with them. I didn't make them breakfast. I made her do it. She would get so pissed about it too. I wasn't their mother, and I wasn't a mother myself. I was a young teenager. It wasn't my responsibility to wake up with other people's kids and change their diapers, put clothes on them, make them breakfast, and do all of the things a parent should do. It was the parent's job.

Treating a kid like an adult or even treating a teenager like an adult by giving them responsibilities they're not emotionally or psychologically ready for can cause the child to bury their anger, grief, or resentment that rears later in life. I myself avoid responding to situations in relationships as well as not knowing how to self-soothe and bury everything because that was what I was told to do. Parentification can cause complex PTSD with symptoms like shame and guilt. I couldn't feel anger toward my parents for the treatment I went through, and even to this day still love my parents deeply even though I am one fucked up bundle of psychosis. Admitting the neglect and abuse was one of the hardest things I did, even when I was coming to terms that it was abuse.

Just like everyone always said and still does, the mistreatment became my own self-blame and my own self-guilt because I was lazy and didn't listen and had I just done everything exactly as they told me to, then I wouldn't have had problems. I was compliant and walked on eggshells, and that was the praise my mother gave to others because I wasn't a problem child. I became a people pleaser from it and rebelling against being a people pleaser has been extremely difficult to do.

My dad was always volatile with venomous words whenever he was angry or drunk or high on pills, and there were many occasions I remember him yelling at both my mother and me because we were useless. I blamed myself for their marital issues because "I was lazy and didn't listen." Their relationship was far from perfect and far from doting. I do know they did love each other. My dad ended up drinking himself to death along with his pill addiction just eight years after my mother had died. He was never the same after she died and was even suicidal himself. He tried to overdose on blood pressure pills. He tried to shoot himself, and the gun jammed. And he didn't have a problem laying it on me that I was his problem of wanting to commit suicide. I sat in the living room one night with him after he had taken the pills, where he said no one gave a damn about him and only used him as I pleaded with him to allow me to call 911. In this state, you have the right to die; consequently, unless he wanted to go to the hospital, they couldn't force treatment on him. After about twenty minutes of me crying as I listened to everything he said about how horrible of a child I was and how he deserved better children than what he had, he finally let me call 911.

When we lived with my father, I was once again his servant and only what I could do for him mattered. I drove to get his pills. I got his liquor and beer for him. For the first time in my life that year, he sat there and snorted his pills in front of me. I was twenty-three. He had always hidden it or made me go into another room. It all changed that year. Later, throughout the years, I would still be his facilitator. When no one would buy him his liquor, I or my husband would go get it. The last time was just a few months before he died. He ended up staying at his mom's house because no one wanted to put up with him drunk. My youngest was just a month old, and he ran me to death that weekend, driving to his mom's house to bring him liquor and snuff. My siblings said I was an awful person for allowing him to treat his mom like that and getting his liquor, but I obeyed what he told me to do. It wasn't long after this incident that we had a huge spat during one of his drunken rages where he was bitching about where we chose to put our woodpile for the wood stove. It was a heated argument, and I didn't speak to him again until he was conscious on life support in the hospital right before he died.

I read the words spiritual orphan, and everything clicked because where I wasn't physically abandoned by my parents and family, I was emotionally abandoned. I always compare my life to others and feel misunderstood and alone in the world. I once wrote, "What do you do when you want to go home... but you're already there?" and uncovering insurmountable different things in psychology and therapy has helped me answer that burning question. I am a spiritual orphan much akin to the black sheep of the family.

Dear Diary,

My entire childhood, I grew up believing we were poor. It's what I was told. Both of my parents were on disability without jobs. Throughout my childhood, until after I turned 18, I had no idea my dad sold drugs and that we were illegally rich. My dad didn't have less than $100,000 in his safe at all times. My parents gave my siblings money whenever they needed it. They paid for their Christmases, shelling out an easy five grand for each of them, as well as buying Christmas for our big family and cousins. I didn't know what it meant to be on disability and had no idea how much my parents' checks were until I was filling out my FAFSA for college. It was then that I began to question how we afforded everything we had.

Don't get me wrong, my parents bought me stuff whether I asked for it or not. My siblings often say I am the spoiled child because "I got whatever I wanted," but honestly, I never really asked for stuff and the reason I got what I did get compared to what they did was because my parents had the money. I am fairly certain I was in elementary school when my parents began selling their pain medication for money. It's very... I don't even know the word for it, but to find out that your family was only legally poor but had ass loads of money.

My dad helped fund my brothers' businesses and helped buy everything they needed for those businesses. At the same time, it rubs me exceedingly raw because my parents refused to give me money to go to college and expected me to solely go to college based on grants, scholarships, and student loans when they could have easily helped me go to school. It was then my responsibility to pay the loans back, which I still drown in because the associate degree I got and the college I went to was bullshit, and I couldn't get a job with my degree and schooling.

In every single aspect of my life from how I was raised down to financial help, my parents always helped my siblings but never me. I lived at home through college, and they bought me my first car, which all my siblings always got a vehicle passed down from our mother, and she would get a new one. She didn't want to give up her car, ergo they bought me a used one on payments from a guy who worked at a car lot. They paid for my insurance on the car and then used that against me for financial abuse. Me living in their house meant to my dad that I was still obligated to do whatever they said even though I was an adult, like cleaning. Or for my mom saying I had to be home at certain times, and I still wasn't allowed to even go to my brothers' houses to hang out. I was an adult and still being treated like a child.

So, my whole entire existence and identity that I felt growing up being told we were poor and, therefore, me not wanting to ask for stuff made me feel like my whole personality and who I was as a person was a sham. It wasn't my lie that I was living, but I had still been living a lie. But it did build my character for who I am today because I live an honest life. We live paycheck to paycheck, and I don't feel like I am beneath who I was growing up or my life downgraded. I am frugal and don't spend much on myself unless we have extra money. Even then, I won't buy myself stuff but usually buy for my kids.

Day Twenty-One
Dear Diary,

Can you have seasonal depression when you have actual depression? Of course, throughout the year, I have my days as a shut-in. I lock myself away from the world that I feel sees me as this atrocious person just because of the way I look. I still talk to people, and I'm my usual self, just going through the motions to seem normal. More to the point, there's a timeframe for me when the days are bad. From around December toward the end of January, I am manic, which is pretty much the opposite of winter seasonal depression. Starting around the end of January and lasting upwards through April, I feel lost. I feel the loneliest a person could ever feel. I feel despair and woe, and it deepens into a numbing feeling that outweighs anything people would say to me to make me feel loved or important. During this time, I seriously recluse myself. I stop talking to people. Those motions of normality become a foreign notion and my soul feels more exposed than at the time of its combination with my body. I am raw and wounded, and every little thing deepens the scars of my past. Past traumas flare into existence, and it's all I can think of.

This type of depression is much different than the depression I feel throughout the year, much the same as the mania I experienced right before as well. It feels amplified. The same can be said for my seasonal depression in the summertime as well. Around the end of June or the beginning of July, I start to feel the mania, and insomnia kicks in. The mania is quite worse in the summer, with the depression not being as bad as in the winter, whereas in the winter, the depression is far worse than the mania. I experience the mania on and off throughout the year as well. The mania and depression dynamic are the signs of my bipolar disorder. When coupled with the feelings of seasonal depression, it is the worst experience of the year for me.

I can't exactly remember the first time I experienced mania. Depression and anxiety were a pretty good norm throughout my childhood and into my adulthood. Looking back, I believe I may have been in high school when mania began to settle as I spent my summer vacation not sleeping through the night and turning into a night owl. I always put this off on it being summer vacation, but it quite possibly could have been me responding to seasonal depression's summer mania. I do know that because of my mania and extreme anxiety, anything that acts like a form of speed, such as the mini thin diet pills that were popular in the 90s or Phentermine, increases my anxiety and mania to further extremes.

When I think of how to explain the anxiety I feel, the only thing I can think to say is it feels like literal waves of tingling electricity coursing through my body, and my heart rate increases because the feeling isn't a normal or natural feeling. It can disorient me and make the room feel spinney. It causes heart palpitations. And if I let it get out of hand, it leads to panic attacks, both normal and extreme. There have been nights where I refused to fall asleep during my mania because my anxiety was so bad it felt like my heart was going to stop beating whenever I closed my eyes. On other nights, when I do fall asleep, I would wake from sleep in a full-blown panic attack, much like veterans have with their PTSD. I can't breathe, and I vomit. My skin is hot and crawls and itches.

Dear Diary,

When I first met my husband, literal stars were in my eyes. I was twenty-one years old. He was gorgeous, something I had never had the chance of experiencing in my romantic life. But I always had the nagging voice in the back of my head of why he was interested in me. I wasn't pretty. I was grossly fat. Even my sister made a sly comment about him being out of my league because of his looks. He was fit and had tattoos. I liked the way his voice sounded when he talked. Something about him soothed my inner turmoil.

We met on Myspace even though he only lived seven minutes away from my house. He had not grown up in the area. He hadn't attended the same school as I did, with all the laughing faces that pointed and snickered at me and my weight. He treated me like a real girl. Our first date was at Subway. He arrived late, and I thought I was going to get stood up. Turns out, his headlights' lightbulbs went out one right after the other, and he had to replace them. I shyly ordered my food and nibbled on it as we sat and talked. My body dysmorphia made me believe that if I ate around him, he would think I was a fat slob. We spent around an hour there eating and talking. It was supposed to have been dinner and a movie, but he was using his parent's vehicle, and they were demanding him to return home in it. So, we finished eating, hugged, and parted ways. I was abundantly glad that he didn't try to kiss me on our first date.

I didn't hear from him much after that. A casual text here and there, and then they stopped altogether. I was miserable. I had once again failed at what was supposed to be easy and normal. I spent a day with an ex and realized during the time there that he really wasn't for me either. But nothing was going to bring me down that month. It was graduation time. I had earned my associate degree and was ready to see the world. I planned a trip to a theme park for college graduation with my best friend/ex at the time, who graciously paid for nearly everything. On the last day there, I sent my goodbye text to both my ex and the guy who apparently had no interest in me. I was going to move on from a once again failed attempt at romance.

In a span of a year, I had dated four guys. One of them was a friend. The other two had been guys I had met on Facebook. I talked with the second one for about six months, the one that I lost my virginity to. The third one was a complete dick. He only wanted one thing over and over every time we hung out, and I wasn't ready to give my body away to someone without emotional attachment. I had tried and failed at this before. He stopped seeing me. I was emotionally wrought. My mother had died in February, and I was trying to cope with the pain through any means necessary.

About a week after the trip to the theme park, my now husband texted me from a new number. Something had happened to his old phone. We agreed on a second date. He was once again late for the date, and I was getting discouraged. However, he showed up, and we went on a movie date. I had already watched the movie, but I didn't care. It was a good movie, and I got to spend some time with him. The movie ended, and he walked me back to my car. And then it happened. He kissed me. And it wasn't just a kiss. It was a moment. I let myself go and fell into the bliss. It was something I had never felt before. I didn't have a lot of experience kissing. My first boyfriend was just chicken pecks. My second one, we kissed but there wasn't any passion. I remember one time opening my eyes during the kiss to see him making some face as if it was the most boring thing in the world he was experiencing. I had never felt the rush of a kiss like I did with him. It was like time stood still with him. He was the one.

We spent the upcoming days and weeks talking on the phone. One night, as we talked, he asked me to be his girlfriend, and I said I would love to be. Our next date was the following day, and it was at his house where he lived with his parents. We went upstairs and watched some movies. He pulled my face into his and kissed me again. Even though I had promised myself that I wouldn't have sex with just anyone I dated, my body told me otherwise. The sex was mind-blowing, and I spent the night there.

At the time, I was in between places living. I had been staying with my brother after my mother's death. I couldn't live in the house after she had died. She died in the house. Plus, I didn't get along with my father still. However, my brother and I had a falling out over his wife. So, I had all my stuff packed in my car and would either spend the night with my sister, my other brother, or spend the nights at my dad's house. I drifted everywhere, not feeling welcome anywhere. I felt like a burden to everyone. I didn't have a place in the world for myself.

I was supposed to have gone off to college, but due to a miscommunication between the college I received my associate degree at and the college I was transferring to, I wasn't able to attend for the upcoming semester. I made plans to sign up for the next semester's opening. All of that changed after I met my husband. It wasn't the first time I had sacrificed college to try and keep some form of familiarity. My mom was the reason I didn't go off to a university or college.

Since I had everything of mine packed away in the backseat of my car and my trunk, he moved me in with him. I woke up one day to find him unloading all my stuff from the car and carrying it into his room. Everything felt perfect until he was injured at work, and they fired him. He entered a dark period. There was one day when he was having a conversation with me and said he didn't feel right continuing to be my boyfriend since he didn't have a job. I didn't care he didn't have a job. I wasn't with him because he could buy things. I had been bought things for years to replace the love of my parents. I wanted love and I was stark raving mad for it. I broke down. Another person didn't want me. Who would want me when I looked the way I did?

He wiped my tears away and kissed me. We didn't break up, but we ended up separated with me not allowed to stay at that house anymore. I had to move back in with my dad, who really didn't even live at home. He spent most of his time out of state doing what he had always done. I was alone most of the time. It's such an odd feeling. It's like having one foot on the side of death and one foot in life.

Dear Diary,

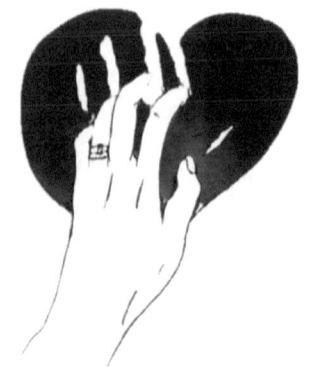

My scars are invisible. I would rake my nails down my skin, bringing blood, but it left scratches and not scars. But the pain is still there. Every time I felt anxious, I would scratch myself. I would chew my nails to the quick. And every time I raked my nails down my skin, I imagined it as a razor. Once, I used the sharp end of the protractor for geometry to make my scratches. It wasn't because I was afraid of the pain that I didn't use a razor. People ask less questions. Scratches can be easily explained away. A cat scratch, a dog scratch, scratching too hard at itchy skin. Not to mention, I feared how my mother would react if she found out. It wasn't death or harm from myself I was afraid of, but what she would do.

I would take bobby pins and shove them into my skin. Not to make me bleed, and I didn't draw blood but just because I was bored. Random little things like that I didn't realize constituted self-harm. Like for instance, I went through periods of anorexia nervosa and bulimia nervosa. I would either starve myself or binge and purge. That is considered self-harm. I have bit my fingers. I chew on the cracked skin around my nailbeds. I rip out hangnails. I have chewed my nails into the quick. I would pick at scabs to watch them bleed. I have rubbed burn marks into my skin with my fingers. I would play bloody knuckles with other kids. I have raked my hands down brick walls to scratch them up. I got my tongue and nose pierced the same day, and they refused me any other piercing because of trauma shock to the body. I sat through tattoos that hurt my sensitive skin. I got sunburns on purpose. I have picked off moles and skin tags. I have a spot on my scalp that I have continuously picked at for years since I was a child. I have punched walls until my knuckles hurt. I play with the fire of candles letting it burn my fingertips and with the candle wax. I have taken scalding hot showers to burn my skin. I would drink mixed drinks to the point of crying because it would induce vomiting. I have choked myself. I have carved words into my skin with my fingernails or a pencil.

I was deep into self-destructive behavior. If I wasn't doing it to myself, I was thinking about doing it to myself. There were countless times I have thought and got lost in the thought of the moment of driving my car off the road into a tree or telephone pole or guardrail, off a bridge, into the water to drown. I have wanted to take knives and dig them into my wrist and slice so far down that death would be within minutes. I have wanted to cut the fat off my body. I have watched myself in my mind pick up a gun and blow my brains out. I have thought and nearly acted upon smashing my hand in a car door.

During my senior year, I became borderline Munchausen and hypochondriac. Whenever I was injured, my mother acted in concern. When I fell in gravel, she would clean my wounds and put a bandage on it. I wrecked my bike once, and she rushed me to the ER, thinking it was broken. I had chronic stomach problems since I was a kid, so she was taking me to the doctor. I had my gallbladder removed when I was seventeen. However, I was depressed and tired. I didn't want to go to school, but if you missed x amount of days, no matter what your grades were, they failed you. I made up excuses to go to the doctor. "Oh, there's a mole I am concerned about." Mom told me to go to the doctor. "I have a sore spot behind my ear." Mom told me to go to the doctor. But then there were also times I fixated on the problems I was going to the doctor over. "Maybe that mole might be cancerous." "What if it is a tumor behind my ear?" "What if my bruises and tiredness are cancer?" The history of my mom telling me to go to the doctor over minor implications had settled deeply into my subconscious where everything seemed like it was important for the doctor. The same day, I went to the doctor over the spot behind my ear, and she took me to get my nose and tongue pierced. I developed an unhealthy inclination toward self-diagnosis because I was self-aware of my Munchausen and hypochondriasis.

My period was severely dysregulated. I was overweight, so of course, that was their suspicion, or just my period hadn't regulated, and I needed birth control. Since I was fat, they overlooked any other warnings or cause for concern that was due to me having an unhealthy eating regime. The periods of starvation would lead me to binge eat, and then the guilt and shame of eating so much would lead to me purging. There have been times I have thrown up so much that food burned whenever I would eat that hardly had any spice to it. I didn't eat at school for fear of being made fun of for doing a basic bodily function. If I did eat, I would sneak and eat and hide, only eating in front of people I truly trusted. I associated food with all my problems. My mom would be nicer to me if I was skinnier. People at school would be nicer to me if I were skinnier. But no matter how much I purged or how much I starved myself, I only continuously gained weight, which would only spiral me into more self-loathing, more self-harming and more self-destructive behavior. There were times I would antagonize my bullies so I could hear the insults because those insults were metaphorical knives plunging into my skin. Had those around me actually paid attention to my behavior, they would have seen the attention-seeking psychiatric symptom I had developed.

When I lost my virginity, it was with a guy I barely even liked. I wasn't attracted to him, and he made me feel awkward the first time we kissed because, honestly, I didn't want to. But I was starved for affection and starved for attention. I was a twenty-year-old who had only ever had one relationship, and it was just two months and one of those months was spent dodging me mostly. I wanted to be wanted. I needed to be wanted. I reached out for it, and it obliterated what little self-worth I had because even someone I thought wasn't attractive at all had not wanted me.

After we broke up, I was on this website that rated your looks and all. Guys from all over the country would talk to me and flirt with me. They would talk sexually to me, and of course, I would talk the same shit back. I even met up with someone from there that I had gone to high school with, and we fucked without any type of strings at all. We didn't even talk after, but I used my body as a way to connect with someone whether we connected or not. I felt shameful about it and guilty. I felt dirty. But it wasn't something I could control. It was impulsive and shallow and at the time, in the moment, I didn't care.

I have often told people that I am shallow, and they have replied to me back that I am indeed not shallow. Shallow people do not acknowledge that they are shallow. Shallow people lack empathy and compassion for others, whereas I show empathy to others. I am deep on an emotional scale because I feel so wounded, but if I had not experienced the type of abuse I had while coming of age, I wouldn't be as connected to my inner emotions. I use my abuse as an excuse. It seems to be the center of attention. If someone mentions they were abused, I jump in with mine, too. Is it a deep connection I am looking for? Or am I just seeking to be the center of attention and to see whose abuse was worse? If I am not the center of attention for people, I begin to think that they do not like me due to my social anxiety.

Since I was allowed to wear makeup, I have been obsessed with it. I obsess over my clothes. I obsess over my hair. I obsess over my overall appearance and want to look presentable whenever I am around people. I have a driving inclination for this obsession. Could my social anxiety and abuse from peers have led me to a narcissistic obsession? Even though I obsessed over my appearance, I did not feel as if any of the things I did made me look pretty. I still had self-esteem issues as I layered on makeup throughout my day. Even though it was narcissistic to check the mirror every so often and reapply the makeup to look good, deep down, I was still not too fond of the way I looked. I dressed according to whoever I was trying to be friends with. I remember once I wore black lipstick borrowed from a friend to a school dance. My mother hated black lipstick. So, before I was to be picked up, I had wiped it off. A teacher who was chaperoning the dance and disapproved of the lipstick made a snide comment about me not wanting my mother to see what I had been wearing. I didn't know the repercussions I would suffer by going against what my mother approved of my appearance.

Any type of attention I would receive from people became my main focus in life. Social media is a cesspool of fake emotions, and I dove headfirst into the murky waters in 2016. It was as if I was God to them online. People flocked to add me as a friend. My life seemed larger than normal to them, even though I was poor. I was a shut-in. I had bad behaviors. I had poor self-esteem. I didn't have any in-person friends. But I was a person of power that they respected. I was deviant in nature. I friended people to become popular. I friended them to seem cool even though I was a loser. I couldn't afford to pay bills on time. I often went without a phone because we didn't have the money to pay for phone service. But the online world was my new obsession. I couldn't leave my newfound popularity behind when it was just beginning.

However, all good things come to an end, and those who are thought to be friends were just as narcissistic as I was. When they no longer had any need for me, they dumped me. I had many personal issues going on at home that they were aware of. It's not like I hid anything from the ones I got close to. They knew that I was spiraling into a black hole of numbness, and instead of trying to help me, they used my weaknesses against me. One of my weaknesses is silence. You can spout off mean things to me, and I will take it blow for blow because I have grown used to it. But silence or the lack of connection really throttles me into darkness. I had a fear of abandonment. Time and time again, those who were supposed to care for me abandoned me throughout my life when I needed them most.

I remember the first time I ever had a nightmare I could remember the next day. I was four years old. In the nightmare, my parents had died, and I was forced to live with my grandparents. I had nightmares of where they no longer wanted me, or my mother would die, and I would have to live with someone else because my father didn't love me enough to raise me on his own. I had a fear of abandonment so deeply seeded that I was having nightmares about being abandoned and had no idea what caused it. Each time I came across a person who left me or stopped speaking to me, that abandonment issue would kick in, and I would drown in loneliness and despair. This rock bottom feeling would always drive me to self-harm because it's how I released my emotions.

Dear Diary,

I watched my sister get beat for three days. I was seven or eight years old. I blocked most of it out, but there are certain things I can recall. I remember my mother jumped on her back to bring her down to the floor and then started beating her with her fists. She beat her so much that she broke her pinky finger. She tried to drown in her dirty dishwater as my sister stood in the kitchen washing dishes. I wanted to stop my mother from hurting her, but I was little. I was scared. I would have been next. As I think back, I want to say I called out to her to stop, but in all honesty, I still feel frozen in fear, not understanding what was happening between my mother and sister. I just knew my mother's lashes were painful.

I grew up listening to my mother say how terrible of a person my sister was. I equated perfection with punishment. If I were perfect, I wouldn't be punished. I didn't sneak out of the house. I didn't smoke. I didn't do drugs. I didn't do anything to step out of bounds. I was an AB honor roll student. I knew the penalty for stepping out of bounds or acting like a normal child. Punishment. In Kindergarten, I watched the movie Buffy the Vampire Slayer. One of the scenes caught my attention, and I tried the maneuver on a fellow classmate. I told him to look and pointed at something that wasn't there, and when he did, I punched him, just like in the movie. I was punished in class, and the teacher wrote my daily progress report, putting an N for citizenship. When I got home, my mother found the progress report for the day and angrily asked me what I did to receive the N, and I told her what happened. I was punished for it and whipped with the paddle. I never hit anyone in school again.

Why didn't I try to run? Why didn't I try to cover myself? It was simple. We had to stand there and accept our punishment, or there would be more lashings. We weren't allowed to cover our bottoms, and if we did, she would hit our hands, and it didn't count as a whipping. We were also indoctrinated that kids listened to their parents, and when you misbehaved or were disobedient, punishment was the discourse. You didn't disrespect your elders. So, there was no fighting back against any of the lashes.

I remember throwing a toy at my nephew, who was four years younger than me, and it hit him in the head. When he cried, she asked me what happened, and I told her. She picked up the toy and threw it at me. It hit me in the face. I was punished for what I did. I never threw anything at him again. He bit when he was going through his terrible twos. His mother bit his arm back to teach him no, and my mother told her she was wrong for doing that. I watched my sister-in-law look at me and said he wouldn't bite me again.

Like my mother, unless I am smiling or laughing, I have a resting bitch face. My mother was yelling at me in my face, and I was standing there taking it. I didn't say a word, but I was slapped across the face and told not to look at her like that. My glasses flew across the room, so she began to tell me to take my glasses off whenever she was going to smack me. It's harder to control the way your face looks all the time than most people think.

We had renters who lived down the hill and had kids the same age as I was. I would often play at their house. The little boy who lived there never listened to anything his mother said, and she never whipped him for it. I remember one time he punched me in the eye and nearly broke my glasses while bruising my eye. I ran home and told my mother, and she insisted on his punishment. He was grounded. I was mad that he was not hit back. It wasn't fair that in every instance in my life, I had something to another child that I had been punished with a hand or a paddle, but he was not. I did not understand that it was child abuse. I did not understand that I was wishing child abuse on another child.

Dear Diary,

No one can ever walk through my mind and see every memory that lives rent-free in my head. No one can see the moments when my mother told me to call CPS, and when they left satisfied as they had with my sister, she was going to beat my ass for calling them. No one can see the moments when my father told me he would never allow me to escape and leave like my sister had and that he would fight for me to stay imprisoned in that house to do what he told me to do. No one would ever see the want to run away and also the fear of what would happen when I was brought back and punished for it.

I wanted to escape my life so badly that I dreamt of dying. I dreamt of running down my wrists. I dreamt of downing a bottle of sleeping pills. I dreamt of stepping out in front of vehicles. The older I get, the more drastic the suicidal ideations have become, like driving my car into a tree or telephone pole or picking up a gun and blowing my brains out. Things are much different now than they were then. I now have responsibilities. So, when the worthlessness is triggered, I must cry it out and keep it together. I have to repress those urges. It will be a long time before I am ever fully healed from what happened to me and shaped me into the ball of anxiety I am today. I have passed one milestone for being over a year, close to two years, panic attack-free.

Arguments and yelling at me severely trigger my fight-or-flight anxiety. I immediately walk from wherever I am and begin cleaning the kitchen, whether it needs to be cleaned or not. There are times I have stood there and washed counters down that have already been cleaned because it's my OCD reaction to stress. My whole world has been nothing but pain and me trying to make it day to day without people asking me questions. I ask many questions to myself, but I dare not provoke the questions outside of myself. Several teachers throughout the school had asked those questions. "Are things ok at home?" "Are you ok, or do you want to harm yourself?" "Are your parents abusive?" I dare not speak the truth for fear of the repercussions of what was to come if they found out. I saw the reaction to my depression and suicidal thoughts, and it wasn't anything loving or caring. I saw what happened when my sister called CPS on my mother as well. Nothing happened. I slipped through the cracks. She slipped through the cracks. We were failed by those who were put in place to protect kids from the harm that my parents inflicted on me.

You don't have to be hit for you to experience abuse. You don't have to have visible bruises or scars for you to be abused. Bruises and scars are evidence of abuse, but that does not mean you aren't being abused. If you are made to truly fear your parents, that is abuse. If they verbally abuse you by calling you names or yelling at you all the time, telling you that you are worthless and good for nothing, that is abuse. If they tell you ugly things about the way you look that make you cry, you are being abused. If they make you do things you don't want to do that aren't safe or normal things, such as drinking a cup you are made to believe is pee, that is abuse. Abuse comes in so many forms and fashions and isn't always physical. If you are trapped inside and not allowed to go anywhere unless it is with family that is permitted to take you places, that is abuse.

Everyone processes trauma in different ways. Everyone processes their experiences in different categories, and some are more perceptible to events they consider to be traumatizing than what others believe it to be. So, you didn't have the hell beat out of you all the time. Well, then, you weren't abused. But that is not the case for every person. Every person has their own breaking point, and what I experienced growing up was my breaking point.

I was around 14 when I started going to church, and I was only allowed to go because our neighbor offered to take me. She was a sweet old lady that lived across the road from our property where we stood to catch the bus. Going to church was one of the few liberties I was allowed. Church allowed me to go to camp for a week. It allowed me to socialize with other people outside of school. I sacrificed church for my mother after she had another heart incident. I had been blamed for a car accident because she had taken me to school, so I knew if something happened while I was at church, I would be blamed for that as well. The sacrifice of church turned into me sacrificing school as well. I didn't go off to school and instead went to a local community college. Not to mention, my father wouldn't give me money to go to school. I would have to apply for scholarships and even more loans than I had to go to the local school. There would be too many questions about where the money came from if he gave me money to go to school. The fear of my mom dying kept me tethered to her even though we never really spent much time together while I was growing up. I hid away in my room, where I felt safe. At night, my dog wouldn't allow anyone in the room without trying to attack them. I was safe in there. It was hard for me to get close and have a mutual relationship with my mother because of the way she treated me. I had overheard her once telling my sister she didn't understand why she couldn't have a relationship with me like she had with my sister. My sister was able to put her abuse aside and maintain a relationship with our mother.

My mother spent most of her time sleeping. On days that she would have planned to go do things with me, she couldn't be woken up due to the medications she had taken, or at least that's what my dad always told me. There were many times he would be angry with her as she fell asleep sitting up on the couch. Once, she was walking around the house in a sleep-induced state trying to cook and dumped out water all over the kitchen floor, which I had to clean, and then I had to cook dinner. She once fell asleep half bent over on the couch with a lit cigarette and set the carpet on fire, which woke her up, and she immediately extinguished.

My sister often says I was allowed more freedom than she was. I wasn't allowed to go on field trips that were long distance or left the state. Friends weren't allowed over other than one of the teens whose mother rented from us, and she mainly came over to see my sister. I wasn't allowed over to friend's houses until I was in college. My first homecoming I wasn't allowed to go to even though my sister went to hers. My sister was allowed to have her boyfriend over. She had friends over. I wasn't even allowed to spend time with my nieces or nephews who lived down the hill. What little bit of freedom I did experience was when I was in college, but I still had a curfew. I was called so many times one night asking when I would be home, and I couldn't leave because of the storm that was ripping through the county. Through her persistence, I left even before it was over and nearly wrecked my car going home.

The day I graduated high school was a similar situation. My parents told me how proud they were of me. When I got home, there was a graduation cake on the stove. I asked when the party was, and my mom scoffed at me. I was chastised for thinking that I should have a graduation party. So, since I wasn't having a party, I told them I was going to a friend's house for their party. A bunch of us were getting together and chilling one last time before summer break and college. I was given a curfew to be home so I could cook dinner. This was the same curfew I ended up keeping for a long time, except the time always changed depending on what the activity was. I had to be home by 6 PM that time.

My mom had promised me a graduation present to go to Dollywood earlier in the year. My choir class was taking a field trip there, and I had raised all the money I needed to go on the trip by selling candy bars throughout the school. My mom told me that everyone was planning on pooling money together for me to go after graduation. When it came time and I had graduated, it had all been a lie. No one was saving money or giving me money to go to Dollywood as I had been promised. So, the free field trip she made me skip never happened for me and I still have yet to go to Dollywood.

The only thing I had was school as an escape. I did well in school because school was my distraction from home. Even through all the bullying, I was able to flourish academically. My father had told me so often that I would be pulled from school and made to stay home so I would have the time to clean. I kept my grades up so I could stay in school. I wasn't allowed a job with them, claiming it would take away from their disability. So, by the time I had graduated college with a degree, no one would hire me. I was green with my degree and overqualified to work anywhere else. I couldn't even get a job flipping burgers at McDonald's because of my lack of experience. I tried working at a bar after my mom had died. It had just opened the same month, and I was hired immediately. But the stress from there added to my depression just made the experience terrible. I quit after about four weeks employed there.

Dear Diary,

Chronic bedwetting. Chronic bedwetters are children who haven't had the biological response to hold their urine in their sleep. The doctors explain it like a switch that hasn't switched on yet. Usually, by puberty, the child has outgrown this biological impairment. I was a chronic bedwetter until I was 16. Now, when the doctors speak of the switch that hasn't turned on, they mean the child never goes a night dry. Every single night, they have wet the bed. When the child has some nights dry and some nights wet, then they start looking at other avenues other than a biological component that is causing the bed wetting. Sleep apnea, sexual abuse, or just abuse in general is usually focused on.

I was a chronic bedwetter to my family. However, there would be days that I would wake up and have not urinated in my sleep and thought that today was the day! I stopped wetting the bed. The next morning, I would wake up in a wet bed. I was already into my puberty age, still wetting the bed. I hadn't seen a doctor since I was a small child about my bed wetting. Had I gone to the doctor and told them I was still wetting the bed, there would have been more cause for concern because I was over the typical age for it to still continue happening. Considering I had dry nights alongside wet nights, it was no longer due to a biological component that I was wetting the bed. It was anxiety.

When your child is a bedwetter, they are already ashamed of themselves. Punishing them, shaming them, mortifying them, and telling other people to mock them does not help them overcome their bedwetting. It makes it worse. It turns their anxiety on every night before they fall asleep because it isn't their fault. They can't wake up to go pee because they don't feel the urgency to wake up or have the capacity to hold it. I was called lazy, nasty, filthy, and all sorts of names for being a bedwetter. My parents were ashamed of me for being a bedwetter. I was ashamed of being a bedwetter. Do people really think that kids want to wake up cold and wet? It feels gross. It is gross. We are already ashamed of ourselves and guilty that we couldn't wake up to go use the bathroom. I was punished in various ways to try and get me to stop wetting the bed. I was paddled. I was degraded. I was told I was drinking urine to trick me into not doing it again. My mother showed me my sheets and told me she had wrung them into the cup before making me drink it. Just falling asleep was an anxiety for me on top of the normal anxieties I felt throughout the day.

My mother bought an expensive bed reversible, pillowtop mattress for me. She figured a new mattress would motivate me to stop wetting the bed. I was cussed for ruining a new mattress that she paid so much money for. I was too old to be wetting the bed, and she never let me forget it. By this time, I was washing my own clothes and my own bedclothes. She never knew when I had dry nights or wet nights unless I told her. I did the whole no liquids after a certain time, stopped drinking dark soda, the whole shebang. When I stopped, she attributed it to the light soda helping me stop. My anxiety had hit a base line that I could cope with was the real reason.

When my daughter turned out to be a bed wetter, I told everyone to leave her alone so that she would grow out of it on her own. She was not allowed to be shamed or punished for something that was completely biological. I wasn't going to let her feel the same way I had felt so often because it was horrible. I bought her pull-ups. She threw them away herself. She didn't have to hide them to fear being in trouble. She had a mattress protector. I let her ride it out. The doctor confirmed the switch thing hadn't been turned to on yet. Then, one day, she stopped peeing in the bed when she wasn't around people who made a big deal out of it. She didn't have the added stress prolonging her switch from being turned on. She was proud of herself, and I expressed that I was proud, too, even though it was never her fault that it was happening to begin with.

136

Dear Diary,

I make excuses for people treating me horribly. My dad yelled at me so much that when I am yelled at now, my first reaction is to go clean the kitchen. But had I just cleaned more efficiently, I wouldn't have been yelled at. At least, that's what I have been told. I was lazy. I was the one cleaning while my mother slept, and my father sat on the couch drinking. I was lazy. It was my sole responsibility to cook and clean while others dirtied the house. I was lazy. That's what I am told.

I was depressed. I was bipolar. I had seasonal depression. I had anxiety. I was bullied. I was suicidal. I was lazy. But all those reasons were not an excuse. I didn't have an excuse to not be able to clean a whole house from top to bottom while going to school. I didn't have an excuse to not be able to come home from school and clean then cook and still do homework. Homework wasn't as important as housework. I was up at 6 am, going to bed at 10 pm and trying to fall asleep before midnight, and I wasn't allowed to take a nap after school, no matter how exhausted I was. As soon as I walked through the door coming home from school, I had no rest. I had to clean. My parents were only taking care of me financially. I was taking care of them full-time when they were able-bodied.

Lazy is a trigger word for me. I have been told for so long that I am lazy that no one has ever taken into consideration the whys. I can spend all day long cleaning just to turn around and have to clean the same exact mess the next day without help, without appreciation, solely expectation. If you speak with my family, all they ever remember is me never doing my chores. If I wasn't doing my chores, my mom wouldn't let me go to my sister's house to clean her house for her for money while there was a house for me to clean. And when I returned from my sister's house a day or two later, the mess that was there was my responsibility to clean all over again.

I remember one time, my preacher decided to stop by the house to pray for my mother's health, and my mother was angry because I hadn't folded the clothes on the loveseat yet. There was a time when the US Marshalls walked through the house looking for my cousin in hiding. Had our house been as disgusting as everyone made it out to sound, they would have called CPS. Other than the few times my mother paid my cousin with a pill to clean our house, I was the one cleaning it, and usually, the times she paid him was because he was jonesing and begging her to give him one, and then he would clean the house for her. She didn't proposition him for it because I usually cleaned the house. He asked her for it. And he wouldn't stop asking please until she caved. And then, when he didn't clean, I would get yelled at for not cleaning by my father because it was a secret that she gave him a pill.

This was my life, even through college. I had to still cook and clean for everyone even though I wasn't home. I was a full-grown adult who still had chores. I was out of the house by 7 am and coming home around 11 pm to 12 am because my classes ran until around 10 pm, and I had a long drive home at night. I was overwhelmed. I was expected to do these things still because that had been my life since I was 10. It went from the kitchen to the kitchen and bathroom, to the kitchen, bathroom, and living room, to where everything was my responsibility to do. However, I was lazy even though the entire household running was resting on my shoulders, to be done.

I used to see my husband as a narcissist. My husband used to be the person who held no accountability and blamed everyone else for why his life went wrong. I often heard the words "I own you" and "You are my servant. That is your job." Many of the phrases he would say to me were the exact things I heard as a child growing up with narcissistic parents. I was their servant. I was their slave. And I didn't escape the abuse until I was 20 and only after my mother died. My husband didn't communicate with me but would talk to others about what he should say to me. I often felt discarded throughout our relationship. I felt unloved, unwanted, and alone through much of our relationship. My husband came from a toxic family, much like I did. He witnessed how his father treated his mother and was taught this was how things work in a marriage. My husband was not born a narcissist but rather molded into one. He used all the behaviors of a narcissist, like gaslighting and manipulation.

Many times, I have felt like I was at the end of my rope with him and unable to escape the way I had when I escaped my parents. But as I stated, my husband USED to be narcissistic. My husband has the same values as I do when it comes to family. I stayed through everything because deep down, I knew it wasn't his fault. I knew it was his upbringing. I knew that other people had taught him how to treat his family. My husband realized that he was not the best person he could be, so he worked on himself. There are moments he slips into another state of being, and that same vicious person with words pops up, but I also recognize those moments are during his anxiety, depression, and other varying mental illnesses arising, and I cannot fault him for that. I rage. I slip into moods due to my own.

So now, we have conversations about his actions. We talk about how what he has said or done is wrong, and he strives for better. And it's not ass-kissing or trying to make me feel better for what he did or said. It is genuine work. There are many men who are reformed narcissists or have recognized that they have a narcissistic trait or personality but are not entirely narcissists. They are the ones that you see telling other men how they are acting is narcissistic. If you aren't safe, no, you shouldn't stay in your relationship. And verbal and emotional or financial abuse is the same as physical abuse. I am not endorsing sticking it out as I have. I have abandonment trauma, so I latch onto people and let them abuse me and rarely leave the toxic situations, but I have left quite a few. I could see my husband struggle. I could see my husband working on himself. I could see he wanted to be the husband I needed and wanted. And I know I am not perfect either, and he has to put up with a lot of stress I put on him as well.

I did not see that kind of growth or behavior when looking at people in my family. I also recognize a lot of the things that I feel toward my husband are trigger feelings from when I was a child and treated in the same manner. It isn't his fault that I have triggers, and it isn't my fault either. It also isn't his fault that I don't keep a line of communication open with him when something bothers me and instead bottle it up like I was taught to do as a child because I don't always tell him how I feel. I don't always tell him when something bothers me, if I am anxious, or if I am triggered because it's never mattered before in the past with others.

Dear Diary,

One of the most basic jobs an adult has to do is a trigger for me. I hate cleaning. I know a lot of people say that, and a lot of people make jokes about it, but in all seriousness, I am triggered by a dirty house, especially when I cleaned it the day before, and it turns into a wreck by the next day. Why is something so easy to do a trigger? I know most everyone thinks I am lazy. That I have no morals or ethics, that it's my mental illness presenting and in truth, it is part of my mental illness presenting. It's my PTSD. I shut down after all my efforts were for nothing.

As a child, my sister turned sixteen and moved out. My brothers, twelve and thirteen years older than me, had long moved away from the abuse and volatile nature of my parents. It wasn't long before my sister followed in their footsteps, leaving me alone in a house with an alcoholic, drug-addled father and a bipolar, quite possibly borderline personality-disordered mother. Everything fell to me to do slowly through the years. I started washing dishes at eight or nine. Then added the bathroom chore. Then it was keeping the living room clean and, not long after that, laundry. But it was never enough. It was never perfect enough. I felt as if I had to scrub the floors with a toothbrush for my parents to be satisfied with their own princess, Cinderella. Except, I wasn't a princess, and it wasn't a fairytale.

I developed OCD from the stress they placed on me to do the chores. I heard so much yelling and berating over chores that now, whenever someone yells at me, or I am in an argument, I immediately start to clean.

Dear Diary,

In my family, when they see and know you are struggling, they just turn the other way. I don't mean financially because my sister has helped me out in ways I can never repay, but I mean mental health wise. As I touched on the lazy trigger, that's all I have ever been called by family. They never took the time to ask me what was wrong or how I was feeling and expected me to perform regardless, even though our mother was a prime example of what depression looked like. I was busy fighting to stay alive, to act normal, to float along day to day while inside; I wanted to die. And I don't mean just a stray thought here and there. Every single day, I thought about how easy it would be to just die. I wouldn't feel meaningless or worthless. I wouldn't feel like I couldn't do anything right. I wouldn't feel like I ruined everything in my wake. I wouldn't feel like everything I touched turned into shit.

I wanted to be somebody in this world. I wanted to go places and see things. I wanted to experience life. But unless my mother agreed to it, I wasn't allowed to experience it even as an adult. Sure, when I turned eighteen, I was given a longer leash to do things. I went on dates with guys, but I wasn't allowed to go to my brother's house and play card games with everyone. I was allowed to go to college, but I wasn't allowed to go shopping at the mall unless it was in between classes. I was allowed to buy clothes, but only the ones my mother approved, which left out tank tops and spaghetti strap shirts because my arms were too fat to wear those. I was allowed to go to a friend's house, but when my mom called and told me to come home, I had to leave right then and there. I was going to work out with my sister and had to stop that because it took away time from helping with my mom, even though my sister was paying for me to go with her. I had a leash and just a taste of freedom, but I, as an adult, did not have total freedom.

I couldn't jump in my car and go anywhere I wanted to. My mom told me she paid my gas and my car insurance, so I was only allowed to go and do things that she said I could. Even when I had money of my own from student loan leftovers, I was still controlled by what I could use it to do. My parents gave so much money to my siblings whenever they asked without them HAVING to pay it back, but my mom bought me clothes once, and she expected me to give her the money in return for buying them, which I told her I would, and I did.

I had one good friend throughout college that I spent time with, but if she wasn't around, I was usually alone doing things. So, there were days in between classes when I walked around the mall alone or watched a movie at the theater alone. I got lunch alone, and after my mom had her stroke, I spent that time catching up on sleep in my car because I was exhausted.

Many of you reading this probably think that everything I say is justified since my parents paid for stuff, and I didn't. That I was lazy for not having a job and paying for my own gas and insurance. But I was not allowed to have a job. I had no financial freedom. I was a week away from turning 21 when I got my first job at a local bar. I was only allowed to get this job because 1) my mother had died that month. 2) I wasn't living with my dad but was living with my brother. 3) While living with my brother, I didn't have the responsibility of taking care of everyone's mess and only had to take care of my own mess, which was limited to mainly my bedroom.

While living at home, I wasn't even allowed to paint or decorate my room the way I wanted to. My mother bought home interior to decorate my room with. When I moved in with my brother, I asked him and his ex-wife if I could paint my room black. They both agreed, and I excitedly went and bought the paint to do my room with the money I had made while working. My sister-in-law and I spent all evening painting it black, and I took colored paints and left handprints on the walls, piece signs, hearts, and spray paint marks. I decorated it how I had always wanted to express myself. I painted why so serious on the outside of my door. I was so ecstatic that I was allowed to do what I wanted to do. When my brother saw what I had done, he didn't express anger, but he wasn't happy. He didn't expect that I was being serious when I asked if I could paint the room black. I apologized and said if I didn't think he was serious, saying yes when I asked, I wouldn't have done it. I felt like I had disappointed him. I tried to paint over the words on the door, but those words are still visible to this day, no matter how many white coats of paint are applied to it. I left my mark on it and whenever I see that door, I smile because that was the first taste of real freedom I ever had.

Dear Diary,

I wasn't allowed to sleep whenever chores needed to be done. There were hundreds of occasions when my father would wake me and yell to get up and clean while my mother was asleep on the couch. When I was in middle school, I had a virus that spiked a fever and caused body aches, headaches, with lower back pain. I was up all day and all night in pain, trying to break my fever. The next day, I was finally able to go to sleep. My father came to my room to wake me up to clean. This would happen quite frequently throughout my life. My sister was having her third child, and the only babysitter they had was me since everyone would be at the hospital. I was up all night long with her crying toddlers, and when I finally got them to sleep, it was daylight outside. I laid down to sleep alongside them when my father came home yelling at me to get up off my lazy ass and clean the house.

My mother was sick with bronchitis, and I contracted whatever virus she had that caused it. I slept on a blow-up mattress in the living room so that I could help her if I needed to. I was up all night with her, and once she fell asleep, I fell asleep, too. I was woken up and told to get up off my lazy ass and clean. I was never allowed to sleep when my body was exhausted. I had to clean when I came home from school. I couldn't take naps after school. If I did, I was lazy. I was having hypoglycemic issues, where my sugars were dropping for no reason at all. This was mostly due to my eating disorder, where I skipped meals all the time. I was tired from it. I was yelled at to get up and clean during one of my sugar incidents, and that was the one time my mother yelled back at him, saying I needed some orange juice from the store or a candy bar. My sugar level was 56 when it was checked with the glucometer.

If I wasn't up keeping the house clean, I was yelled at repeatedly. I was the ONLY ONE cleaning it. My siblings call me lazy to this day. I was lazy for not cleaning up after every single person who came through that house and dirtied it. I was lazy for not cleaning every single day, doing what my mother was supposed to do. I didn't have one chore. I had them all. I didn't ask for these chores. They were assigned to me. It was my responsibility to keep everything clean. When I started college, my mom started paying my cousin with pain pills to clean the house because I wasn't home to do it. He would take the pain pill and not clean. The school I went to, I usually spent all day there in classes. There would be times when they were spread out through the week, but usually, I was up for school at 6 am, and I didn't get home from school until around 12-1 am due to the drive home. Once again, since I wasn't home to do the chores, my father yelled at me. I was over 18 being treated like a child. And one day, I had it. He told me I lived there for free and ate their food for free so I could clean their house. I told him I was his daughter and he let other people live in that house for free before and I had to wait on them and clean up after them when they could clean for their keep as well. I was going to move out. My mom had a stroke. I refused to go home to that house, though. I stayed in the hospital with her the entire time she was there, and when she left, we stayed with my brother.

It was three days before she died that we moved back in with my dad. He said he would help her if she needed it while I was at school, and the night she died, he told me to go out and have some time to myself so he and Mom could spend time together. I went to the movies with a friend and got home around 11 that night. I was tired and emotionally drained and ready for bed. I was having boy troubles with an ex, the same person I had gone to the movies with. Mom told me things would work out just fine as she climbed into her hospital bed. That was the first night that I had pure and true freedom without someone telling me I needed to come home. That I couldn't go anywhere because I needed to clean. That I couldn't go anywhere because I needed to cook. I was allowed one day, and then my mother died.

Dear Diary,

Normally, once the Winter solstice has come and gone, a buzz is felt in the air. It's an energy that feels suffocating, like a blanket wrapping us in the atmosphere and I would remark something wicked this way comes. As a survivor of trauma and mental illnesses, they say that we are more empathetic. We can read the energy of a room. I felt like I could literally feel the earth slipping into its final resting state before spring arrives to bring it all back to life. It was easy for me to succumb to this feeling and sink into the feelings of death. It felt like it would take me over. Once my mania peaks, insomnia kicks in, as well as extreme anxiety, then depression settles in. I once described the feeling as drinking coffee laced with cocaine and also eating a 50,000 mg edible. You feel like you have all the energy in the world throughout your body, but at the same time, you feel like you can't move from being paralyzed through anxiety. You want to get up and do stuff, but you're in couch lock.

This feeling is exhausting. It's frustrating. It makes you feel like there is nothing you can do to stop it from creeping up into your spine. I used to just accept that it was a part of me, and I had to learn to live with it, which is true. It is a part of me, and I do have to learn to live with it. But learning to live with it doesn't mean you allow it to take over your life. I would wallow in my seasonal depression and bipolar disorder. Seasonal depression hits me twice a year, once in the winter and once in the summer. The winter is the brutal version for me. I experience everything almost as if it has tripled, and the depression that comes along with it is completely crippling. During the summer, the mania hits around mid-July, and I have some insomnia and a bit of depression, but nothing like what I feel in the winter months.

When we moved to our new house in 2019, I stopped letting my mental health consume me. We also started doing more things as a family. During the summer of 2020, we started going camping a lot. It was peaceful to be out in nature without a care in the world. Sure, there were people around, but it's not like going group camping where everyone just walks to your tent space when you're trying to vibe and ground yourself through the energy from earth. People are there to enjoy their own camping experience, so no one really bothers you. My husband and I had finally had a chance to spend some much-needed time together that had been foregone in the past. The out-of-town job he had kept for three years had put a lot of strain on our marriage, and we started to build it back once he got another job. Camping was what we needed the most. Well, what I needed the most.

I don't like leaving my house. I keep my curtains drawn. I am a very private person, as well as paranoid and isolated. Social services had been involved a couple of times in terms of my housekeeping and house repair upkeep. Several of those times, I was working full-time and didn't want to come home and have to clean my house as well. It's already exhausting since the work I did was as a certified nursing assistant in a nursing home. My husband didn't really help other than taking care of our oldest child. I was pregnant the first time they were involved, and the whole experience was traumatic for me. We had left our daughter with my seventeen-year-old niece, who was living with us at the time, so she could babysit her while I ran to the DMV. My daughter was two, and I didn't want to be left alone with her. She wanted to come, but I didn't want to fight with a two-year-old while waiting and having her wait with my husband in the car seemed excessive, so my niece volunteered to watch her. As I got into the car, I sternly told my niece to make sure she watched her, and she assured me she would.

She had her boyfriend over and wasn't paying attention to my child and she got out of the house. She wandered down our long driveway to the main road and was chasing a cat up the street when someone found her and called social services. It didn't take long for them to figure out whose kid it was when the 911 report came in about my niece being in danger. She had also told my husband that she had lost our child, and he had sped home angrily. I wasn't there to witness anything, so I don't know what happened, but it was said that he had threatened her with a gun, and they called 911 to report him. It had been over an hour at this time, and no one had reported my child missing.

We had just moved back into my parents' home to live from the apartment we had in Roanoke. It needed repairs, and that was a big concern for them. The other concern was the mess in the house. I was eight months pregnant, working full-time and had no help from anyone staying there. But of course, I was always the blame for a messy house. When we lived at the apartment, I had to clean on my days off. I did the same when it came to the new place. We got the house fixed up and cleaned up, and everything was fine. Flash forward a couple of years, same story different scenario. I heard that my husband's parents had been calling social services on us. Little did I know that they had been reporting us to social services for years at this point, me being the one at fault for the reason our house didn't stay clean (much like my childhood and adulthood growing up). I had enough and told my husband I was going to stay with my sister because I wasn't dealing with the bullshit anymore, and he could come, or he could stay. He chose to stay, and I left. They had been babysitting the kids while my husband started a new job, and I continued to work, and then suddenly, they stopped keeping them and I had to change my work schedule. So, when I moved to my sister's house, they no longer saw them at all.

After I left, they called social services on us again after my son was hospitalized sick. It was my choice to have them keep him because he had been throwing up a lot and was running a fever. This still persists through today and he is being tested to see why he has these episodes. Not only did they call social services, but his dad also called the cops, saying he had our oldest with him and was drinking and doing all kinds of drugs and everything. After this happened, my husband also abandoned his family and moved. We met with the social services lady at my sister's house and prepared to rent a trailer from my sister. I quit my job to stay home and take care of our kids. While working, I was always on the go and was able to work through my mental health issues. I worked the second shift, so the overpowering exhaustion wasn't as bad since I could sleep in through the morning.

However, when I became a stay-at-home mom, my depression crippled me. This was when I received the diagnosis of being bipolar. I cleaned, but I didn't clean all the time. There were times I let the messes through the house go for a week before I cleaned. I kept the kitchen clean because I cooked every night. The laundry piled up, and I would have to spend two days doing that. Having two toddlers running around the house isn't as easy as some people think it is. My sister should know considering she would pay me or my twin nieces to come clean her house because the mess would also pile up there as well. After drama over living there, when my husband got a new job (he was working for my sister and her husband at the time), we were evicted and locks changed on the house. We broke in, got our stuff, cleaned up the mess in the house, and were homeless for a couple of weeks until we could get back into my parents' house.

I found out I was pregnant not long after we got settled back into our old home. Sadly, the baby didn't develop, and I was a bit crushed since this was my third miscarriage. My husband's parents moved in with us and things were going smoothly. The house stayed clean and everything. I was in a good place mentally and pushed forward out of the funk the miscarriage had put me in. Then I became everyone's workhog again. I would wash dishes and all and clean up in the mornings and when my mother-in-law would get up, she would bring dirty dishes from their room into the kitchen, so I had more dishes to do. I wouldn't touch them. I had already cleaned for the day. She would get a pissy attitude that she had to clean the dishes and started to disrespect me in my own house. They lived with us rent-free and not having to pay bills. They put cable and internet in, and that was their bill to take care and I was ok with that as long as they kept the bill paid. They canceled it and still didn't chip in for anything while living there. They lived there for about six months when they moved out to live with their oldest son and his boyfriend. Their staying there had started to stress me out, and I never once asked my husband to ask them to leave because we had lived with them before, and I was returning the favor. However, it stressed me out with them living there. There, of course, was drama when they started moving, but it all passed. Once they moved, everything started feeling normal again.

The following month after they had moved out, I found out I was pregnant with my third child. My husband started a new job, and things were good. My oldest started kindergarten, and my second child and I got to spend quality alone time together through this period. During this time, I became a published author and a publisher. All the stress began to take a toll on me, though. My husband's job was out-of-town work, so I was alone throughout the week. Around the 13th week of my pregnancy, I started bleeding and cramping like I had done with my very first baby. I was distraught. I had a book release the same day I went to the emergency room. I was so scared I was going to lose my baby and have to deal with that trauma I had dealt with six years before. I had a tear in my placenta and was ordered on bed rest until a doctor took me off. I was on bed rest for the entire pregnancy since I was at high risk with gestational diabetes already, and I was having blood pressure issues. I tried to keep the house clean. I would sit in a rolling chair and roll around cleaning up the mess even though I wasn't even supposed to be doing that.

During this time, my mother-in-law died, and we all felt it deeply. Everyone was depressed over it. My father-in-law moved back in with us because he no longer had the money to keep his trailer because my mother-in-law's disability paid for rent. My house stayed clean, and I cooked even though I wasn't supposed to be on my feet. It was during this time that I hit a low I had never felt before when I found my husband talking to his ex (again, after I had already talked to him a couple of years before about not liking it even if she was a friend of the family). I was emotionally distraught and was due to have my baby in two weeks. I spiraled. Depression set in heavily, and by the time it was time to have the baby, my upkeep of the house had slipped.

After the baby was born, c-section like the other two, I ended up having to be the one to clean the house even though my husband had been home from work for a week. Things began to pile up as I healed from surgery and took care of our newborn. I began to sink into postpartum depression. I was doing everything alone. I was basically a single parent that had someone paying the bills. Several months later, my father died as well. Spiraled isn't even a word that could describe what happened. I lacked all the motivation to even get out of bed. By 2018, I was suicidal because of my mental illnesses and stress. I was constantly oversleeping and my oldest missing school. I would clean once a week. My second child was ADHD and autistic (his diagnosis came a few years later). It was extremely rough on me. My husband still worked out of town. We had marital issues. Everything was taking a toll on me.

Social services got involved again, and we went through the court systems because of my child missing school and the issues I had with my second child. He was late with potty training, mostly by pooping on himself, which was later discovered to be a stomach issue (and the stomach issue most likely stemmed from food allergies). My kids lived with my father-in-law while we once again tried to repair the damages to the house that they required us to do. We ended up in a car accident, and my husband was out of work for two months. The repairs fell behind both because we weren't physically able to do anything and because we didn't have the money either. I was in constant pain with my neck and back, which I still suffer from from the accident. During repairs, we found that the house was beyond fixing. My husband and I hit the hardest point in our marriage, and I told him he needed to find a new job, or I was leaving because I couldn't put up with the stress anymore. He found a new job, and things began to feel better. Once we got our settlement from the accident, we bought a new place and moved. Social services were in my life through the middle of the pandemic when they decided that everything was good in our household. It would have been sooner, but I had pneumonia in October 2019, and during one of the checkups, I hadn't cleaned up for a couple of days (and they didn't care I was sick).

One thing that was the takeaway with it all was that the courts said that even though I was the one at home, there were others who acknowledged the mess and didn't help. The courts knew I struggled with my mental health and said that when people saw me struggling with my mental health, they should have helped. It wasn't my sole responsibility to clean. It wasn't a total excuse to not have cleaned, but there were other capable bodies in the house that could clean and didn't. They empathized with my struggles, and for once in my life, I felt seen and heard. Someone recognized that my mental health paralyzed me, and it had taken a heavy toll on me. I couldn't do everything alone, and they validated that and said that it shouldn't only be me doing everything. Since I was a teen, it had always been just my responsibility. Even when I worked. Even when I had surgery. Even when I was sick. Even when I couldn't physically do the cleaning, it had been my responsibility. And they said that wasn't fair.

No one else in my life sees it this way. Everyone expects me to perform. If I don't perform, I am lazy. However, I am not lazy. I have been fighting to survive every single day of my life for as long as I can remember. Everyone says that suicide is selfish and that people should fight through it, but no one ever helps those who struggle when they see them drowning. Not a single person offered to help me throughout my entire experience of depression throughout the years. No one ever volunteered to come help me clean my house. Instead, I was lazy. No one ever checked on me to see how I was doing when I was stranded without a vehicle to use.

My sister-in-law and nephew that lived down the hill fed us when we were hungry, took me to the store when I needed to go, and to the doctors or the school and all. But no one ever asked me if I needed help. They only judged what they saw. I was lazy because I wouldn't clean even if I physically wasn't supposed to or if I mentally couldn't perform.

I spend days cleaning now. I have tried teaching my kids chores, but they have heard for so long that it's my job to do it, and eventually, I will clean what they refuse to clean that in the end, they don't do anything. And it is so exhausting to be stuck in this cycle of perpetual blame when no one offers to help take care of me. I need to be taken care of at times, too. I need someone to take care of me when I am sick or when I have depression. But I take care of myself and push through like every mother is taught to do like every wife is taught to do. Stay-at-home moms are not stay-at-home slaves. It is not their sole responsibility to take care of the kids and housework just because someone has a job. We cook, which is a job. We clean, which is a job. We take care of kids, which is a job. We care for the sick, which is a job. We have multiple jobs that aren't being helped out. A partnership should be 50-50, no matter if only one person is the financial support in the relationship. I was the financial support of two children. When the kids were sick, I took off work to take them to the doctor. When the house needed to be cleaned, I was the one to do it. When the baby woke up at 3 am, and I had to go to work at 5 am, I was the one changing the diaper and feeding the baby. I helped when I was the financial support, but I don't get the same energy returned to me at all. I know my husband struggled with depression, and I didn't fault him for it. However, I am always faulted for it. I am always the one to blame for it, and it is not fair. I know life isn't fair, but when you try to equate things in terms of fairness, such as it isn't fair for me to work a full-time job and come home to have to do things, then yea, I am allowed to say it too because I DID. I came home and would cook dinner if it wasn't done. I would come home and take care of the kids. I would come home and clean. I did so much while I worked.

So now, when my house is a wreck, I check the windows for cars pulling in because I am paranoid. I don't like visitors because all they do is judge without asking questions. Why is my house a mess? Because I have been trying for three days to get my kids to do their chores. I have been trying for three days to teach them they have responsibilities. But that doesn't matter to anyone. I am the one at fault. My kids are old enough to know how to throw stuff away and wash dishes, swap laundry, clean their bathroom, clean their room, etc. But they won't, and I have to do it just so no one will talk about me behind my back, or no one will call social services, and social services won't step in to tell me how I am to blame for the mess in my house. If I am the one responsible for the mess in my house even though my kids are old enough to do chores and help, then I was not responsible for days as a kid or as a teen or even as a new adult when I had yet to do my chores and clean for my parents. If it is my responsibility now, then it was my parents' responsibility when I was a child, too, except everyone places that on my shoulders as well.

My chores never went more than a day behind while I was a teen. I would get in trouble if they did. I have been the blame for so long that I feel the blame is mine. I loathe myself for going through episodes where my housework gets out of check. I call myself lazy. It's what I have always been called, so it must be true, right? I learned at a young age that it didn't matter what you were going through. No one cared. They only cared about what you did for them. And if you couldn't perform the way they wanted you to, you were worthless. You were useless. You were lazy. You were a sloth. You were trash. It takes two seconds to ask someone if they are ok. It takes two seconds to ask if someone is struggling. It takes two seconds to care about someone other than yourself. It takes two seconds to find out if you need to help someone you love. In my experience, no one has ever cared long enough to ask me these things, and no one has ever cared to help. In my experience, the only hero I have ever had to save me from me has been myself and fear. I live with fear locked away in the attic of the mansion within my head. But fear has its own key to the door. So, it lets itself out and brings with it anxiety, depression, and every other symptom of my mental illnesses that live rent-free in my head. And I battle them all entirely alone. It is so lonely and frustrating being me.

But even as I struggle with all the blame, both mine and others, I still have to remind myself that I am not lazy. I am mentally ill. My mind controls my actions, not my body. I am trying to stay alive.

Dear Diary,

I don't think you can ever escape abuse when it is prevalent in a household. I have woken up to slamming doors, shouting, fighting, and many other things as secondhand abuse. One night, I was woken up by my father yelling and shouting about the police coming. He had tried choking my mother, and my sister intervened and then called the police. Like most narcissistic abusers, his thought process was the same. It was my sister's fault that he had to leave and be gone before they arrived so he wouldn't be arrested. He shifted blame from himself to her to make her feel guilt at the thought of him being locked away would inevitably be her fault for calling for help. It was the same tactic our mother had used on us when she abused us both physically and mentally.

But those things weren't the sole reason for me being woken up after I had gone to sleep for the night. I remember once my mother had gone shopping and left us at the house alone. I woke up to someone I didn't even know trying to rape my sister. When I walked through the house, he was running out the back door because my mother had pulled in after returning from her shopping. I never knew if she told my mother that night, but I do know it was disclosed to her at some point.

I watched how men treated the women in my family, and it was rooted deep in my psyche. Couple that with the constant abuse I received from boys at school, and I feel totally uncomfortable around men I do not know. I have a constant fear that something bad could happen to me, even more so when I am asleep. The panic attacks that happen when I am asleep have an unknown root cause, but I know it was at the hands of abuse that happened prior to and during being woken up. What specific abuse I cannot say because I do not know. I do know that I was told by a doctor that panic attacks and anxiety attacks like to strike the hardest when your body is relaxed, which sounds completely opposite of what one would think. But it also makes a lot of sense because I was caught off guard a lot with my abuse. When it was least expected is when it would happen.

I don't even remember what would lead up to me being smacked across the face, but what my mother would say right before that is don't give me that look. I have come to learn as an adult, I have a resting "bitch" face, so even when I don't mean to look a certain way, I look like I have an attitude.

Day Thirty-Three

Dear Diary,

I have been trying to understand my mental illnesses for years. Through childhood, I didn't understand my mood dysregulation at all, and even through adulthood, I have never understood the whys until I started researching.

During mania of bipolar affective disorder, your serotonin increases and your dopamine increases. During the depression phase of bipolar affective disorder, your serotonin decreases as well as your dopamine decreases. This happens in a cycle. But what happens during the times that you aren't in a bipolar cycle? I have researched the symptoms of high and low serotonin and dopamine and have found that I oscillate between the two of them. Like for instance, social anxiety is a symptom of higher serotonin levels as opposed to lower, but general anxiety and depression are listed as a symptom of lower serotonin levels, which has been refuted in medical studies saying that depression is not directly caused by serotonin at all, and there is no correlation between them.

Dopamine, serotonin, and all the chemicals that control our bodily functions are a daily cycle and follow a circadian rhythm. We have a natural rising and lowering of our chemicals throughout the day. These chemicals are responsible for our sleep/wake system. Serotonin helps the pineal gland create melatonin from melanin to help us naturally fall asleep; however, serotonin also promotes wakefulness through the production of norepinephrine. Dopamine suppresses norepinephrine, which allows us to fall asleep. Any type of imbalance between the two will cause sleeping issues. Dopamine imbalances cause depression, and serotonin imbalances cause you to not be able to process your emotions. These all reset daily. However, if you are having issues with imbalances, the daily reset isn't going to go to baseline each time.

So, what exactly are serotonin and dopamine then? Serotonin is a chemical that carries messages between nerve cells in your brain. With that said, most of your body's serotonin is created in the gut. Serotonin plays a key role in such body functions as mood, sleep, digestion, nausea, wound healing, bone health, blood clotting and sexual desire. Serotonin and dopamine have been seen to be released by sunlight, but in truth, the sunlight is what gives us vitamin D, and vitamin D stimulates the production of both dopamine and serotonin. That's why many who suffer from seasonal affective disorder have a vitamin-D deficiency. A lot of people with chronic inflammation and chronic pain have also been said to have lower levels of serotonin while also having lower levels of vitamin-D.

Low levels of serotonin symptoms are anxiety, sleep problems, digestion issues, suicidal behavior, obsessive-compulsive behavior, PTSD, panic disorders, migraines, phobias, and schizophrenia. The symptoms of too much serotonin vary from mild to high. When your serotonin is slightly elevated, you are shy. You feel like you're not good enough. You want to be social but also fear it at the same time. You are nervous. You can easily be upset by criticism. You lack motivation. Some more serious symptoms of higher levels of serotonin are feeling agitated or restless. Mental confusion or disorientation. You have headaches. You are dizzy. You have an increased heart rate or blood pressure. Your pupils dilate. You have goosebumps, sweating, or shivering. You experience stomach upsets with diarrhea, nausea, or vomiting.

Dopamine is a neurotransmitter and hormone that acts as your reward center. It aids in many body functions, such as memory, movement, motivation, attention, and more. It is your pleasure and reward hormone. It also controls sleep and arousal. It's part of the network of feel-good hormones and plays a larger role in depression than serotonin does.

Low levels of dopamine symptoms are tiredness. You lack motivation. You are unhappy. You can have memory loss and mood swings. You can have sleep problems and concentration problems. You will also lack sexual desire. Low levels of dopamine can cause ADHD, Parkinson's disease, and restless legs syndrome. Excess dopamine levels can cause high libido, anxiety, difficulty sleeping, increased energy, mania, stress, obesity, addiction, migraines, and improved ability to focus and learn.

When you have just the right amount of dopamine, you are happy, alert, focused, and motivated. Some scientists now believe dopamine's role isn't to cause euphoria like previously believed but to reinforce remembering what is pleasurable. This is why addiction happens with higher levels of dopamine.

When our ancestors were alive and thriving, they relied solely on what they could find to eat, drink, and have a safe space to sleep. This was all controlled by dopamine. Dopamine is released when our needs are about to be met. Since we no longer have to hunt or track for survival, our dopamine depends on relationships with people and our surroundings. The slap on the back for a good job done by people you know releases dopamine. Finishing a project that you have been working on releases dopamine. Engaging in activities that make you feel happy or relaxed releases dopamine.

However, even though the pleasure and reward systems are set up to help us survive, in modern society that doesn't require the basic instincts to live has pushed us into unhealthy habits of pleasure and reward. When we feel upset or sad, we reach out to food for comfort, creating a dopamine release whenever we eat something that we know isn't healthy but tastes good. Sugar, carbs, and saturated fats all help release feel-good chemicals in our brains. The dopamine remembers what it feels like when we partake in these things, and it forms a habit that can lead to eating disorders. This creates a pattern of guilt and disdain for oneself as one begins to gain weight from the things that make them feel good because our body begins to crave the feel-good release from those items.

On the contrary to flowing dopamine from eating the sugar and carbs, low levels of dopamine can lead to starvation, such as eating disorders around anorexia. We find no joy in food because the food we are eating doesn't provide us with the dopamine dump that we need. Then there is the vicious cycle of bulimia, where we find joy in the food but experience the guilt that makes us throw the food up and not eat for several days because we fear the weight it causes.

These chemicals normally work together to make our bodies sustainable each day. They do not act independently and work together each day to maintain our functionality. When one is out of balance, it causes the other to go out of balance. Low levels of serotonin produce high levels of dopamine because serotonin inhibits dopamine production. They affect our appetite, where serotonin suppresses it, and dopamine increases the hormone ghrelin to produce hunger. So, when you are depressed and have no appetite, you have higher levels of serotonin and lower levels of dopamine. Serotonin inhibits impulsive behaviors, while dopamine encourages it through the reward system it has set up.

You are never going to have a solid balance of chemicals that make you the perfect human specimen. I should add that one person's imbalance will never present the same as another person's imbalance. While learning to grow cannabis, I learned that there are three main nutrients, along with a few more in all plants, that are mobile nutrients that could cause a plant to die if the needs aren't being met for those three nutrients. What I also learned is that there is a system of immobile nutrients that, if one of them goes awry, it causes a deficiency and prevents the main mobile nutrients needed for survival from being absorbed. If you compare our bodies to plants, we have the same network of functions. Our main mobile nutrients are a network of seven neurotransmitters. Dopamine and serotonin are two of those neurotransmitters, along with glutamate, histamine, norepinephrine, acetylcholine, and gamma-aminobutyric acid (GABA).

Glutamate is the most abundant of all of them because it keeps our brains functioning properly, with learning and memory as its main functioning roles. Histamine operates the gut, skin, and allergy response. Acetylcholine controls muscle movements. Norepinephrine controls the skeletal system as well as the heart muscle to constrict during your "fight or flight" responses during an acute threat alongside epinephrine. Gamma-aminobutyric acid (GABA) is an inhibitory neurotransmitter and reduces the effects other neurotransmitters have on nerves, such as decreasing anxiety by inhibiting norepinephrine absorption.

During, say, rising anxiety levels, GABA is released so the norepinephrine and epinephrine don't cause overstimulation and result in panic. However, if something is imbalanced, GABA isn't going to be released, leading to an anxiety attack or panic attack. Along with these neurotransmitters come hormones that are essential to those neurotransmitters functioning properly, much like the immobile nutrients of a plant. Like if you don't have the proper amount of endorphins in your system, then the stimulation of euphoria isn't present. This goes hand in hand with dopamine. Endorphins boost the release of dopamine, which allows the feeling of euphoria.

This leads to an important hormone that isn't deemed that important at all when it should be. Oxytocin is the "love hormone." It is released during labor to induce childbirth. It is released during breastfeeding for lactation. It modulates fear and anxiety. It is our natural antidepressant since it stimulates both dopamine and serotonin production. But it is also the hormone that we learn to bond, trust, and love others through. This hormone is released during sex and orgasm. It's released when we are hugged. It's released when we kiss those we cherish. It is released when hands are held. It is released when you smoke marijuana! It helps create core memories.

Oxytocin is detrimental to functioning properly. If you don't secrete enough oxytocin, then everything the hormone teaches us through social interaction and experience isn't converted through dopamine, which stimulates glutamate since it is also a hormone and translates everything into learning and memory. See the domino effect? So, if one of these hormones that stimulates vital neurotransmitters is being released into your system, then that neurotransmitter isn't going to function. So, overloading a person with dopamine and serotonin isn't going to fix a lack of endorphins or oxytocin and lead to long-term effects that present as mental illness. The problem is that most of these vital parts of our body can't be quantified through blood tests like iron or vitamins.

Whenever I am feeling down in the dumps or have no motivation, or I am anxious, etc., I have sex. Even if I don't have the sexual desire to have sex, I have sex. Sex promotes the release of oxytocin. I feel the rush of the love hormone rage through my body. My dopamine increases. Endorphins fire, and I feel bliss. I feel safe in that moment. I feel loved in that moment. My husband calls it emotional support dick. And quite honestly, that is exactly what the penis does. It helps regulate our emotions during sex because, along with the dopamine being triggered by oxytocin, it also releases serotonin, which regulates our emotions and helps process our emotional response.

Over-stimulation or under-stimulation to any of these neurotransmitters will knock your mental health out of whack and, if chronic, cannot self-regulate, leading to long-lasting mental illness. Anymore, when you go to the doctor and tell them I am depressed, all they do is randomly prescribe you anti-depressant medication without looking into why you are depressed. Even when going to licensed psychiatrists to treat your depression or your bipolar disorder, they don't get down into the nit and grit. They just randomly choose medications they think will help you, and many of those medications are dopamine suppressors and serotonin boosters. As discussed, low levels of serotonin overproduce dopamine, and dopamine causes mania. So, if a patient complains about mania, it's automatically assumed they have low levels of serotonin. Well, higher levels of serotonin induce the same manic feeling as well. So, using that course of medication is only going to heighten the mania and can also lead to serotonin syndrome. It could very well be that your dopamine is doing fine or even deficient in the moment of mania because the serotonin is elevated. Deficient dopamine presents as depression and anxiety. You can totally be manic, depressed, and anxious all at once.

I have had migraines since I was a little kid. Doctors now think that a low level of serotonin is the cause of migraines. In studies, it shows that glutamate is increased during migraine attacks. It was also cited that dopamine is used during migraine attacks where the levels drop and then return to baseline post-migraine. However, when there are low levels of serotonin usually dopamine isn't inhibited. Dopamine also increases glutamate. The same diseases that are caused by chronic increases of glutamate, overexcitement, are the same diseases people suffer from too little dopamine. So, if those same diseases are present in both of those situations, then even elevated levels of dopamine wouldn't be the cause of the glutamate surge. This, in turn, shows the correlation between the use of dopamine during migraines, causing lower than normal levels and the increase of glutamate being responsible for the diseases they cause. Serotonin is also directly responsible for stimulating glutamate. So, if both of these increase glutamates, a low level of serotonin cannot be the cause for the increase of glutamate chemically. The actual cause is the sudden increase of glutamate that your GABA neurotransmitter has failed to inhibit.

GABA controls absorption. The bare root of all the neurotransmitter functioning relies on GABA. Stress and other factors can create issues for GABA to function properly. However, GABA also relies on other chemicals to function properly as well. Oxytocin stimulates GABA release. So, if oxytocin is deficient, your GABA will be deficient, leading to a whole array of neurotransmitters misfiring as well as migraines. Even when it comes to hormonal migraines, there is a direct correlation to the drop in oxytocin when the estrogen levels in a woman's body drop. It's not the actual drop of estrogen that creates the migraine response but, in fact, the direct correlation of the drop in oxytocin that leads to GABA misfiring and glutamate rising.

The correlation between oxytocin and GABA also explains why abuse mentally affects people who go through those traumas. Being in any type of abusive situation will cause your oxytocin levels to drop as well as your GABA levels, which in turn causes various chemical responses to fail. Lowered oxytocin creates a fear response, which triggers epinephrine to surge. Adrenaline slows down your oxytocin, making it harder to recover from your fight or flight response. This leads to chronic anxiety and, in other cases, PTSD. Childhood abuse leads to feelings of abandonment, fear, and not feeling loved or worthy due to decreased levels of oxytocin and those feelings are made into core memories. Traumatic experiences during teenage years or adulthood are the same.

Gabapentin is a medicine that is prescribed for epilepsy, neuropathic pain, and migraines and increases the release of GABA in your system. This is what has helped my migraines for almost a year. Whenever I would take serotonin-based migraine medicine, I felt like I was dying because my serotonin levels were fine, and I was going into serotonin syndrome. The use of THC and CBD in clinical studies leans toward cannabis increasing GABA production in adults along with oxytocin release. This is the reason why marijuana is good for pain, mental health, migraines, and a lot of other symptoms that GABA levels control. Now, it isn't the cure-all, and a lot of people say that it makes their issues worse, but it has helped me tremendously overcome many of my ailments since I have used it habitually since its legalization.

Do you know why they call your intuition your gut reaction or say trust your gut? Because that's where dopamine (50%) and serotonin are produced. Dopamine creates your learned responses to scenarios. Paired with other hormones like oxytocin, it helps you learn and compute social behaviors and commit them to memory through the stimulation of glutamate. So, when you're stressed or your levels are off-balanced, your stomach is stressed. The brain and gut are connected through receptors. So, when your receptors are triggered by deficiencies it tells your brain to respond by altering your well-being. When I had my hysterectomy in 2020, things were fine for right about two weeks after. I started feeling what most contributes to postpartum depression because it's been reported many women become depressed after losing the vital organ that contributes to their biological need to reproduce. My surgery left my ovaries so I wouldn't go into menopause early and would get 5 to 10 years before I went into menopause. However, I felt off after contributing it the research on postpartum depression.

But what exactly is postpartum depression, and why does it happen? I have never had a doctor explain it to me, even though I experienced it after my second child was born. Postpartum depression is attributed to the drop in estrogen and progesterone in a woman's body that lowers other hormones, mainly oxytocin. I was never able to breastfeed any of my children because of supply issues. With my last child, I did everything suggested on the market to increase your supply by eating certain vitamins and foods. It didn't help. I firmly believe now that my oxytocin levels were low because, with all three children, I was induced into labor and had c-sections. I didn't have that natural release of oxytocin by having natural childbirth. My hormones were always out of balance, so I was already oxytocin deficient. Having a hysterectomy sent my hormones into chaos since I had a natural imbalance of sex hormones as it was. The sudden drop in estrogen caused my oxytocin to tank as well and induced postpartum depression afterward, which was treated with Zoloft. It made me feel "ok," but I didn't take it longer than a month because it was messing with my sexual desire in the end, and it really wasn't fixing my issues completely.

About a month to a month and a half after surgery, my stomach issues began. I have always had GERD, but I was able to go untreated for my GERD for years up until this surgery. I had so many gastrointestinal issues after the surgery, but my doctors wouldn't listen to the surgery being the catalyst for my issues and blamed it on my weight. Instead of seeing what was causing my sudden onset of symptoms, they sent me to a bariatric doctor who triggered my body dysmorphia. It is two years post-surgery, and my stomach still has issues. I developed a food intolerance to pork. If I eat too much pork, I end up with horrible stomach issues and sulfur burps. When I googled sudden onset of food intolerance, it mentioned estrogen in women triggering it. After learning about estrogen and oxytocin's relationship and then oxytocin's relationship in balancing GABA and other neurotransmitter chemicals, I now firmly believe that I am oxytocin deficient.

A new study has been performed that shows the correlation between babies that have colic and gastric discomfort, linking it to an over production of serotonin because they have yet to create melatonin from the production of serotonin. Those receptors don't start working until the baby is three months old, and the melatonin calms the gastrointestinal tract and is a natural muscle relaxant where serotonin causes cramping in over production. However, babies also produce oxytocin when they are born. They begin to produce it before they are even born. Since oxytocin controls the release of GABA, it can be assumed that the direct skin-to-skin contact with babies that help them release oxytocin stimulates the release of GABA as well for the control of serotonin. So many mothers get frustrated when their baby is colicky and have no idea what to do. They try burping them because they've been told it's a gas build-up, but in truth, those who aren't suffering from an actual lactose intolerance are experiencing an oxytocin deficiency. We have been warned not to pick our children up too much, or we will spoil them. Research now shows that babies are healthier when there is lots of skin-to-skin contact, and one reason breast feeding is encouraged in babies as opposed to bottle feeding is when the mother has the supply and capability of doing so.

My mother had a supply issue, much like I did. She couldn't breastfeed and instead had to bottle feed. My sister also faced the same issues with supply and breast feeding. That is three immediate family members that had issues breast feeding, which can most likely be attributed to an oxytocin deficiency. ADHD, autism, addiction, and mental health disorders are prevalent in my family, leading me to assume that they are genetic conditions within the scope of my family, with oxytocin deficiency being one of the main genetic concerns. Oxytocin deficiency is a symptom of being on the autism spectrum and why those who have autism have poor social skills. I have taken the tests that doctors will review along with their own testing that has determined that I am on the autism spectrum. Doctors say that if you have children on the spectrum, then most likely one or both parents are on the spectrum as well. My cousin's oldest son (on my mother's side) is nonverbal autistic, and my sister's son was diagnosed very similar to my own son regarding the spectrum, scoring right below average on the scale. Another cousin, the brother of the one with an autistic son, was born with cerebral palsy as well as an intellectual impairment. People with cerebral palsy might have mental health conditions, such as depression. Social isolation and the challenges of coping with disabilities can contribute to depression. Behavioral problems can also occur. These are all symptoms of an oxytocin deficiency.

I have heard the stories where my mother would become so frustrated with my crying from my colic that she would hand me off to my second oldest brother for him to bounce me on his knees and try to calm me. Had doctors had the research then that they do now, they may have been able to diagnose my issues better. Even as I am writing this, there isn't much research on doctors prescribing or ordering oxytocin supplements for women who can't produce milk or for fussy babies that have colic. But everything always leads back to the gut with all these chemicals that control our brain function.

I have had GERD issues since I was a small kid. From constipation to diarrhea and throwing up, I have consistently had stomach problems that could be attributed to stress and anxiety. Stress and anxiety are linked to the deficits of dopamine and serotonin, but no one attributes them to smaller deficits that could play a huge part in overall health. Mostly, the symptoms of mental health issues are moreover applied to just serotonin and dopamine level problems and not overall health. People who have chronic pain develop depression after the onset of pain. Chronic pain is a sign that there is a deficiency somewhere in the body, and the aftermath of not fixing that deficiency is the onset of depression and other mental health problems because everything in the body is interrelated. So, in theory, the pain comes from the deficiency that is causing depression symptoms, and chronic pain is one of those symptoms. Something as small as oxytocin can set off a domino effect that leads to a catastrophic outcome of various disorders.

Doctors aren't trying to cure mental health issues. They only mask the symptoms with depression medications like SSRIs instead of trying to get to the real issue that may be causing all the body's issues. They look at depression and GERD as two separate diagnoses instead of something causing them both. You see a doctor for mental health, and you see a separate doctor for gastrointestinal issues, and the issues never overlap in the appointments because that area of expertise isn't studied within the same doctorate program.

After many doctors and many tests, I changed doctors to a new doctor. Within eight months, I had the diagnosis I had been waiting for. I had severe food allergies. These food allergies were causing everything from my GERD to my gastrointestinal upset, my chronic sinusitis and chest infection for two months, which had prompted the allergy test, and so many other things, including my anxiety, depression, and bipolar issues. It turns out all of my mental health issues that were unexplainable, like my seasonal depression from a lack of vitamin D, were caused by malabsorption of vitamins due to chronic gastrointestinal issues. The medicines that made my mental health worse made it worse because I didn't have an actual chemical imbalance that required those medications.

After my diagnosis and stopping the foods I shouldn't be eating, I am entering the new year feeling more alive than I ever have in my life. The chronic tumbling of emotions and thoughts, the numbness and buzzing brain, the brain fog, it's all gone. Of course, the effects of depression and anxiety that I have dealt with for so long still linger. Being depressed and anxious for years never really goes away, as well as the memories of the traumas I have experienced. But I feel like a new person now. What caused my mental illness symptoms doesn't negate the fact I still experienced those things and even went misdiagnosed. I was forced to take medicines that nearly put me in the hospital. I'm just glad that I have the answers I have been seeking for four solid years now. My doctor took all of my symptoms he had gathered over eight months together and presented me with what he thought was wrong instead of blaming it on my weight as the last doctors had. I will be eternally grateful to him as well. My mysterious food allergic reactions to foods I had eaten before make sense now.

Dear Diary,

What does brain fog feel like to me? It's like being on autopilot. You want to do stuff, but you have neither the neurons nor the energy to do it. Want to write? The words are there, but your brain can't piece them together because it's wading through mud and instantly tires you to the point that the only function you can do is aimlessly scroll through Facebook or watch TV. Need to clean? Good luck because your brain is reserving all your energy just to keep your body alive. Think coffee will help? All it does is amp your anxiety, and you're still tired and unable to function normally. Need to do work? Well, those words on the screen Need to be processed and filtered into sentences, and your brain doesn't have the capacity for it because it's telling your lungs when to breathe in and out and your heart to beat. Brain fog is like being on the other side of the veil or in another space of time and seeing people and seeing the world but being unable to interact because you can't ever reach the side you need to be on. It's sleepwalking with eyes wide open.

Someone once asked me what anxiety felt like, and it was so hard for me to put into words what anxiety meant to me because my anxiety is different than others. I always feel late, even when I have nowhere to go. I always feel like something is coming, like a tornado in the middle of winter or like I've done something wrong. Even as I strive for perfection, it's like I'm locked away in a burning room, but no one else can feel the flames or breathe the smoke but me. It feels like my body could vibrate away, and I have to move to remind myself I'm still alive. It's like the reaper has his hands around my beating hard, squeezing the life from me, but I never die. It's like fear has settled into my bones and permanently moved in. And along with fear came panic. And along with panic came paranoia. And along with paranoia came instability. And instability caused irrationality. And soon my reality has become like a dream, and I float along a cloud in a waking sleep. And that waking sleep pulls in numbness. And that numbness brings silence. And I slowly start to go insane as thoughts pile in my brain because I can't feel anything anymore. I'm erratic and nervous. I'm blusterous without ambition, and the knife glints so beautifully in the light until the sound of a baby crying naps me from this sleepwalking state with a message from a friend asking me if I'm alright. And the tears start pouring down as everything rushes in at once. That's what anxiety means to me. Anxiety is the real silent killer.

What does shutting down look like with me? Ignoring the world burning down around me so I can stress-scroll Facebook. Or ignore the world around me through disassociation by reading or watching TV shows alone in another room. I won't talk to you or just mumble, agreeing with whatever you say. Why have I shut down? Because I was triggered either by an argument or something said with spiteful meanness. Who triggered me? Most likely someone I love that had a funny way of showing they love me.

I wish I could say I was like everyone else on the inside. Beating heart, lungs moving in and out. The color red running through my veins, supplying me with life. Even if not that,... just something. An ice-cold heart and the color black to match my dying soul. But there isn't. I am just empty inside, much like death.

My mind is more dangerous than any monster or human. At any moment, it can turn into a killer, and the victim will always be me. I have had so many intrusive thoughts run through my mind. There are days I can see myself dragging a knife across my wrist, and it's like a siren's call... like Sleeping Beauty being drawn to the spinning wheel to prick her finger. Run the car into a tree. Pick a gun up and pull the trigger. The thoughts tell me no one loves me. No one wants me. No one cares about me. I am alone. I am unwanted. It's so fucking exhausting to stay above the thoughts.

I'm trying to exist, but it feels like I have a broken part that keeps leaking my life's essence out through a small hole, and as time ticks away, the leak gets worse and worse. I was once able to laugh and love and now I reserve all my energy for flight or fight, and I have been fighting for years to stay above the pooling excretions of my soul. One day, the tank will either run out... or drown me... I will never be able to fix that hole.

My soul wasn't built for this world. As much love that swirls around inside like a hurricane in the stars that I offer without condition, there's not enough offered to me in return. I skim the surface, grasping only the reef of solitude. People fill the waters, but not a hand do I know. Not a hand reaches for me. I silently bob in between life and death. The darkness of life, the darkness of chains. The chaos of my own mind. As I sit in my chair, in a world full of people who know not how to save.

I have always filled my void with people instead of self-love. I have always wanted to just feel connected to people, to feel what I never felt growing up as a child. I wanted to be needed. I wanted to be wanted and not just a picture on the wall that no one ever notices as it gathers dust. I realized most of the people I have tried to connect to love me no more than I love myself, and now I am slowly weeding out the ones who were truly being selfish. Sometimes heartbreak has nothing to do with what a person has done but everything that person didn't do, and it is heartbreaking when people don't see you for you or know you for you or look beyond themselves to see when you are hurting or when you need help or even just simply say you are wanted and needed. Say I love you or compliment the efforts you have put in. Recognition is very important to feel worthy so you can put the work in for self-care to lead to self-love because I have loved people with my whole being but have never felt it reflected back. I don't know how to recognize it. That's why people will never see the real part of my soul. For it is truly hidden beneath layers and layers of scars that help shield the bruises. The bruises are the only pain that can be felt, just enough pain to let me know I am alive and not dead.

Dear Diary,

Another trigger for me? When people that you love and care deeply about, and they should love and care for you the same, do something that massively lets you down. A trigger warranted by my parents and throughout my life, triggered by others that made salt in the wounds that never healed.

After my sister moved out, my mom stopped going places other than the grocery store or to her doctor's appointments. I touched briefly on how when she died, I couldn't wake her, expressing how it was normal, so I didn't think anything of it until it was too late. My mom would sleep the day away. Sometimes, she would sleep a few days straight. It was a normal occurrence. On the days she was awake, she would make promises to take me somewhere. On the weekends, there was a huge flea market that we used to go to when I was a kid. That would be one of her promises to take me there on Saturday. So, when Saturday would roll around, I would wake up and get ready. It would then be time to wake my mom so she could get ready, and we could go. However, she wouldn't wake up. I would try for hours to wake her up, frustrated and angry, crying she wouldn't wake up because she was breaking her promise to me. It was like this quite often.

I would be alone in the house with my mother asleep on the couch, my father gone out of town, and no one around to talk to. I was raised by a TV set and music, then later a compute with the internet. The internet was my only outlet into the world and pretty much still is. I don't have a strong relationship with my siblings. I don't visit them much, which a lot has to do with distance, but it also still feels awkward to be around them. I still expect to get a phone call whenever I am out and not at home telling me to get home because I wasn't supposed to have left the house, to begin with.

People don't understand why it bothers me so much when plans change and the plans we have fall through. They don't understand that it is a trigger for me because that was my life from age 10. Promises to take me somewhere because I wasn't allowed to go anywhere other than the few occasions my sister would take me to the mall or to a movie. A lot of times, I was a tag long to help watch her kids, like if we went swimming or something.

I never had a family vacation other than when my mother would visit her father in the summer. My brother took me to the beach once with him on vacation, and my sister took me once to Florida with her for vacation. Those were the only real vacations I had other than spending the week at my grandpa's house, where I did the same thing I did at home. I either sat watching TV inside or sat outside on the porch listening to music in my own head or reading a book. I used to love reading until I realized the only reason I loved reading was because it was literally my disassociation from reality because I was traveling in the stories.

All the promises broken, being left alone in a house with no one to talk to, never being allowed to go anywhere or even just walking next door to your brothers' house left an imprint in my mind. It caused abandonment issues. You don't have to be literally abandoned like an orphan to have abandonment issues. No one was ever there for me. No one was ever there for me to talk to about things. If I did talk about things, it wasn't listened to. As an adult, I face the same issues. I don't have close friends that I can just drive to their house and chill. People let me and my kids down all the time by making promises and then breaking those promises by changing their plans. Many times, throughout the years, it has just been me alone in my house with the kids without adults to have an actual conversation with other than online through messenger or text message. So, I seem needy and clingy when there are people to talk to because I grew up without that connection to people, and when I find that connection now as an adult, I cling to it. And even when people leave me by dying, it feels like abandonment all over again.

Just like how my mom wouldn't wake up to go to the places she promised she would take me, she wouldn't wake up the morning that she died. No matter how much I shook her or yelled her name or smacked her across the face, she wouldn't wake up. I was stuck in that time loop for the longest time until I went back to one of the first memories I had where she had promised me to go somewhere and then wouldn't wake up to leave. I went back to that frustrated crying child, and I held her. I accepted her frustrations. I accepted her anger. I accepted her crying. And then it all made sense to me. It wasn't my fault. I didn't recognize that my mother not waking up the night she died was something more serious than any other time I had tried and failed. Every single moment that I had experienced that frustration and anger of those broken promises came rushing forth. Every single time, I begged her to wake up, and she wouldn't wake. Every single time, I would be so frustrated that I just wanted to punch the wall because I was so angry; she had broken her promise to me. Isn't it a promise from a parent to make sure your child is ready to leave the nest and learn to live their own life?

I hadn't been afforded that luxury through manipulation and control for so long that my mother dying was as if she had broken another promise to take me somewhere because I couldn't wake her up. I couldn't wake her up to answer me like always. I couldn't get her to open her eyes to say we weren't doing what she had promised. I was let down by my mother once more, and it wasn't even her fault. And I took the guilt and the blame and placed it on me. But how could I have known? How could I have known it wasn't her normal routine of how she would fall asleep eating her cakes bent over half on the couch with her head resting on the coffee table? How could I have known it wasn't her normal routine of where she was going to sleep for two or three days straight? How could I have known that the night I told her goodnight, love you would be the last time I ever told her those words because I knew even if she didn't wake up right away, she would eventually wake up.

It was such a normal occurrence to me that I had no idea she was dying until I heard the death rattle like the one she had when she had pneumonia. She would open her eyes then, but she wasn't aware or awake but this time, she didn't open her eyes at all. She wasn't breathing right, and she wasn't opening her eyes, and that's when I knew something was wrong with her. That's when I realized that this wasn't the normal occurrence and that I needed to call for help. That's when I realized that mom was going to die. And she did. She never opened her eyes like I expected her to later that day. She didn't wake up apologizing for oversleeping. She didn't wake up at all, and I have been stuck for so long in blame over not calling sooner than I had that I didn't even realize it was because of my conditioning. She had conditioned me into believing that when she wouldn't wake up, she was sleeping and would wake when she would wake up like she always had. Was it normal when it happened during conditioning? I have no idea. I have no idea if it was her medication or if something was wrong, but no one else seemed to find it alarming, so neither did I.

I was a kid. And that kid grew into the twenty-year-old standing over her mother's deathbed, freaking the fuck out that her mom wouldn't wake up and was also breathing funny. That twenty-year-old blamed herself for fourteen years wishing she had called 911 sooner than she had and always felt like everyone blamed her for it. I don't know if they did or didn't. I don't know if recent words were said out of spite and anger or out of truth. But those feelings welled back up, and I was going through that guilt and blame again after hearing it was my fault she wouldn't wake up because I had given her sleeping medication when I had not. It was just what she did all the time and was just a typical day in the house that I had grown so accustomed to. And when I hugged that little girl crying and aggravated over her mother not wanting to wake up to go where she promised, I hugged that twenty-year-old as well, and I told her it wasn't your fault. It wasn't your fault that that had been your everyday experience with your mom, and this one time was when she needed help. It wasn't your fault that she died because you had no idea that it was different than any other time. She had aspirated in her sleep before vomiting. That's how she got pneumonia. It wasn't your fault. And it wasn't my fault.

All the things that have happened to me from my childhood through my adulthood have caused my mind to crack and break. From trust issues and abandonment issues to just simply going to a social event for my kids at school, I have anxiety that just builds and builds and builds without an end. I don't know if there will ever be an end. I hope one day...

Dear Diary,

One of the things I have faced throughout my entire life is the lack of faith in a higher power. So often, I have seen toxic spirituality where people say turn to God to fix your brokenness and your depression, and it is such bullshit to witness. For those of us who struggle so hard to find mental clarity and to peel back the traumas we have experienced, adding in an omnipotent God that allows such things to happen to us is shattering.

The very definition of omnipotence is having unlimited power and the ability to do anything, and yet, people suffer. Many explain it away as God works in mysterious ways or even the whole he carries you through those hard times, through the valley of the shadow of death, for you to see the sun on the other side of things. But for those who have traumas rooted in emotional abandonment, such as me, a presence there is not what we need. We need to feel the love and no matter how hard I have tried to feel the presence of the divine, it always still feels as if I am totally alone. I am so tired of hearing have faith in God because, through him, you will prevail. I don't prevail through him. I prevail through myself. I pick myself up off the floor. I wipe away my own tears. I fight the demons within my mind alone. The one set of footprints in the sand are my own footprints because I carried myself out of the bowels of hell, not God.

I am a wayward daughter because I spent my entire adolescence being controlled, and the blessing of adulthood allowed me to be uncontrollable. I left, and there wasn't a thing anyone could do to stop me from leaving. Even God himself cannot control what happens in my life, and if he has all along, then he is just as manipulative and abusing as my parents were. If he controlled my life, then he knowingly allowed me to experience pain over and over, and what does that say about him? Suffering in silence without a healing hand is traumatizing.

And I have searched for the love and the feel of his presence in my life. I went to church. I read the bible as a teenager. It offered me no comfort and no solace to my plight. I have gone ungrounded and wavering. I have tried to feel the connection of anything and everything. The only thing that seems to soothe me is nature. The colors, the beauty, the smells, the sounds, and the sense of the sun and wind on my face have been the only grounding and calming effects I have experienced. But even those things cannot blast through the troubles that ail my fragile mind. Those things cannot sustain me when I feel lost and need guidance.

The connection I lack isn't with a force that is untouchable and unseeable but a connection with tangible love. I need a connection to people. Connecting with the tangible doesn't come easy to me. I have often said I am not a people person because I was forged that way. Through emotional abandonment, traumas, through social pressures in adolescence, I learned to walk alone. I learned that it was the only way for me to survive because it was how I survived, even though I longed for a connection to the outside world past my little family. I want to make friends, but I am also afraid of losing that connection. I fear abandonment. I fear being left behind. I fear another name being added to my wall of disappointment because I was not understood or cared for as I needed to be. I fear not being treated as a person but being treated as an object that can be tossed away once it is of no use to the person wielding it.

I keep to myself, so I can't be hurt because all I have experience is hurt from those closest to me. I wall myself in to keep others out, but those walls also keep me locked away as well and drowning in memories and emotions of times when I needed someone to break down those walls. I can never be vulnerable around people because my vulnerability leads me down paths where I am destroyed. I always feel I can never be whole or be who I truly am, and people don't really know who I truly am. Even through all the hardships I have faced, I have a bubbling personality that beckons to come out. It wants me to see loudly along with music. It wants me to dance haphazardly in the rain and splash through the puddles created. It wants me to go on adventures and to see the world through rose-colored glass as I did as a child.

But that glass was spray painted black, and light was not allowed inside to awaken my innermost self. I want to love without reason and without rhyme, but I cannot because of what I have experienced. Love has always been my downfall. I love too hard and too fast, and it consumes me in flames of need, but they're only my flames. I do not allow others to add their flames to me because I fear it will burn my world to the ground. I quell the flames and press forward with words billowing through my splintered mind. Words that echo from the past that I would not be loved unless I am a certain way.

The scriptures of religion demand that you be a certain way to be loved by the almighty, and I just don't fit the bill. It always feels like that cascading embrace is never surrounding me, and I am unworthy of love from not only people but from the divine presence, even though I have followed morals and ethics and the words that tell you how to be in order to be loved by God. I reached out to God the same way I reached out for love and affection to those who were supposed to guide their child. I had no guidance, understanding, or compassion, and it is the same way with spirituality for me. If I could find peace for myself from the past, would that open me to the same peace and loving nature that the supreme beings offer? Why do I have to be unbroken and fixed to feel those things? Why can't I feel those things and be loved for who I am?

I have never claimed to be perfect, even though I strive for excellence and perfection. My legs are broken, and I have crawled everywhere I have traveled, trying to beat the odds of my future. It always feels as if something is missing, and I have filled that void with knowledge and everything imaginable to feel complete. My inception was insidious from the beginning, and I have fought for every breath that my lungs have inhaled. But will these things prove I am worthy to anyone? Will these unfortunate mishaps build me as everyone says they do? Am I stronger because all I ever feel is weak? Is that the grace of my soul? I honestly don't know. I just wish someone would wake me from the sleepwalking nightmare where I dream with my eyes wide open.

I hold onto the belief that there will be beauty in all the pain I have gone through. That the flames of my soul will always light the way for me to guide myself to safer passage. Darkness surrounds me in an icy grip of death even though I know I am alive. It still feels as if I walk around within a body that has long been dead, and the only thing keeping it going are those flames within. I hold onto the hope that even though I feel like this today, someday, I will escape this world of everlasting agony. It still doesn't stop me from questioning if there is an unlimited power that can do anything, then why do they let me walk through life in such torment?

I cling to the hope that the darkness will subside and the dawning of light will illuminate the abyss I have been trapped in for so long. That the sun will rise above the valley of the shadow of death and light up the path I have been fighting my way through. That I will make it through everything I have ever gone through during the twilight hours of the night. I am holding on, and that's simply all I can do. Through every high and low, through moments of weakness, through a hero's journey, I hold onto the promise that the light will be there for me when I can't imagine finding a way out of this hell hole. As I drown in doubt that I can make it to the end, I keep believing in the promise of an end.

Day Thirty-Seven

Dear Diary,

No one will ever understand the fear I have of death, especially considering I am also suicidal. It's hard to explain to people who know you have mental health issues and have wanted to commit suicide in the past that you fear death. But it's quite simple to explain away. From the age of five, I grew up fearing at any moment, my mother would die. And then she did die when I was still growing into being an adult. I hardly consider the age I was an adult age. But honestly, at what age do you really become an adult other than legal reasoning? We become adults at the age of eighteen because the government says that's the age, but are we truly adults?

Most people my age are still trying to find themselves well into their 30s. So, twenty is hardly the age of an adult. I would be thirty the next time I experienced a heavy death. It was the death of my father. There have been countless family members and friends who have died, and I fear the death of my family. I worry every day that something will happen to my husband at work. Will he fall to his death from a lift? Will he wreck the vehicle he is driving and die? Will a piece of machinery end his life? And those same fears carry over to my children, too. Are they safe away from me right now? Has their bus crashed? Have they been shot in a school shooting? Did they choke on their food? So many scenarios play over and over in my mind, causing anxiety and fear.

My own mortality plays into my fears as well. What if I die and they're left without me? I am the one who cares for them when they are sick. I am the one that helps them with homework. I am the one who cooks their dinner. I wash their clothes. I tuck them into bed. I do everything for my children. Who will replace me? Will the person care for them the same way I did? Will they be evil toward them? Will they hurt them? Will they feel alone or abandoned because I am not there? So many questions and so many frustrations, and whenever someone close to me dies, these fears and anxieties come raging to the surface.

And along with that fear comes the fear of being alone. Those questions about my husband dying leave me thinking about how alone I would be, how he is the only person who has cared enough for me to stay. And then that leads to the fear of him abandoning me like many others have. What if he were to leave me? I have no one but my little family. I would be all alone to face the world. I don't want to be alone. I have always been alone, and I have tasted what it's like to not be.

There are so many fears and so many anxieties that swarm around in my head that it makes it hard to breathe at times. It cripples me and makes it hard to function. There are days I just disassociate from my feelings and sit in bed binge-watching TV shows and movies just to numb my mind and not have to think about anything. That's the lazy part of my life that people don't understand. I am distracting myself from intrusive thoughts. I am distracting my mind from replaying every little horrific could-be scenario from happening. I am trying not to fall apart while everyone looks down on me with disapproving opinions. But TV, music, and reading have been the only coping mechanisms I have had since I was a child. I was raised by a TV set because there wasn't anything else to do. I read the books to have adventures I would never have. I listened to music to soothe my soul. And then I found the internet to connect to people. It's a triggered compulsion from fear and anxiety, and it is complex trauma that just doesn't go away because I want or need it to. It needs to be healed. It needs to be dealt with. I need to learn how to cope and self-soothe from it. So, if I don't know how to do those things because I was never shown or taught, I go back to the things I do know. These are the escape mechanisms I am used to. And if I don't escape, my mind will eat itself like a cancer spreading through a body.

So, when people ask me what my worst fear is, I can never tell them what it is except for superficial fears. My true fear is fear itself. Fear runs my life. Anxiety works that fear like a ventriloquist performing a show for an audience. I fear death taking the only love I have felt in my life. I fear love abandoning me. I fear the way it twists and gnaws at my insides, creating panic attacks that make me feel like I am dying. I fear every intrusive thought that pops into my mind. I fear fear. And I don't know what or how to respond to that epiphany. I don't know how to not fear fear itself. But I wear that fear like a broken heart on my sleeve in total transparency. I tell people I have fear. I tell people I have anxiety. I tell people I have depression. I tell people I have seasonal depression. I tell people I am bipolar. I tell people I have complex PTSD. I tell people about my abandonment issues. I tell people about my trust issues. But no one ever listens. And everyone expects me to shove it down and just deal with life because life isn't fair anyway. People who are supposed to care don't. And it just plays in a never-ending loop of past, present, and future for me over and over and over until I am suffocated by the thoughts, and I lay in my bed and watch TV.

Dear Diary,

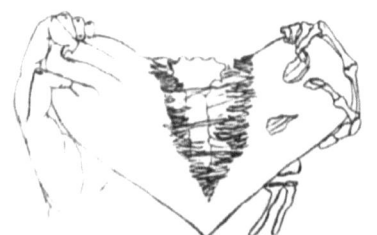

I have always been expected to just "bounce back from it" when, honestly, I just fake it so I can make it. I guess some could call me a fraud. I have often told myself I am a phoenix rising from the ashes of rebirth and renewal, but honestly, I haven't risen. I have floundered in the ashes of the continuously burning fire, and each time I begin to rebuild my form, it is immediately swallowed by the lapping and ever-burning flames of torment and hell that I live in.

I squall in silence from the ever-burning fire. It builds a rage within me that I cannot suppress, but the rage is always against me. I tell myself I can save myself because no hand has ever reached out to help me anyway. But I cannot save myself from the never-ending loop of destruction I wreak upon myself. The havoc consumes my every move, my every thought, my every escaped word. But I do not speak the words of the pain I feel. I bottle them on pieces of paper in a box wrapped in silken guilt and blame and sealed with torment and agony. I want to let the box go. I want to let it all go. But I clutch them like precious pearls because these feelings are all I have ever known. This rage is the fuel that keeps me going.

I have relied on myself for so long that my independence seems stable, but honestly, I rely heavily on the support of others. I need approval from others. I need those words because the words I have for myself are neither nice nor encouraging. I don't tell myself I can do this. I tell myself that I am failing. I don't tell myself to move forward but stay stuck in the past. So, as the ashes of my past are trying to burn away into dust, I reignite the embers and keep them alive.

I am a mottled mess of varying attachments that overlap and intersect because I have experienced it all. I avoid closeness but crave it, at the same time feeling needy and clingy. I don't let people in, but I fake it until I make it. I never feel like I can truly rely on people because they have let me down so much, but I can't rely on myself either because my independence is rooted in trauma and plight. I have the words on the edge of my lips to express how I feel in conversation, but I can't utter them because they have never mattered spoken out loud and only mattered in ink on paper.

So, I burn to rebuild, but there's nothing to rebuild except years and years of repetition. Every rebuild is burned to a crisp because it is flawed so haphazardly that it doesn't deserve the light of day to be recognized. I want to find myself, but I am lost because I don't know who I am. I have never been taught who I am. I have never been reassured of who I am. I cycle through personas. I cycle through ambitions. I am a jack of all trades, but none of the trades ever tell me that that's who I am, and I have found my calling. The only thing I ever hear is that I have failed at just being. How can I move forward when I don't even know who I am on the inside? Am I a good person? Did I deserve what happened to me in the past? Am I worthy of love? Am I worthy of people? Am I worthy of life? These questions haunt me, and I eat them like Wheaties to grow strong, but all I do is grow weaker and weaker as I eat and eat, destroying myself from the inside out.

I am the reason I flounder. I am the reason I am stuck. I am the reason I don't rise because I don't let myself. But do I know how to, honestly? Do I truly know how to rise from the grievances of the past and let them go to move forward with a new purpose and a new directive in life? It's hard to say for sure. I have tried, and I have perished in the flames multiple times. I am always on fire. I leave smoldering footprints wherever I traipse because I was forged in hell, and hell is all I know. I may have climbed out of hell with scrapes on my knees and burn marks on my feet, but I brought hell with me when I escaped from the pit. And that hell reminds me every day of where I came from and where I belong. I may have escaped hell, but it left its imprint on my soul, and no amount of scrubbing can erase the scorch marks that it left. I came from hell, and hell is who I am, is it not?

I have fought so hard not to become my parents. I have so hard not to let how I grew up affect the way I raise my children or affect their own personal views of themselves. I have fought to keep them from feeling those flames as I do each day. The biggest failure of my life would be for my kids to feel like I did as a kid. I felt trapped. I felt worthless. And I felt like I had no home when I was sitting in my room. I felt like an orphan even when I was surrounded by family. So, if I can get just that single thing right about my life, maybe the flames will finally subside. Maybe they won't. But that would be one thing I didn't fail at that I could add to a new box wrapped in golden bliss and open for all to see.

Dear Diary,

Give Heaven some Hell

4-19-1992   9-20-2023

I have often spoken about my nephew, whom I was close to, who became addicted to drugs. We grew up together in a love/hate relationship style, more like brother and sister than aunt and nephew. I honestly consider him my little brother, the one I never wanted. I felt like I was pushed aside when he came into the picture, and jealousy was consistent with that feeling of abandonment. I was forced to share my toys with him, and he was the only kid around really, I had to play with growing up. We were four years apart, and it was a typical sibling rivalry.

His addiction to drugs slowly drove a wedge between us, and I began to feel as if I was being used, as I have always felt with everyone. He went to jail at one point, and when he got out, he moved from the property to his own place to rent. It wasn't long after this that we moved as well. I didn't get to see him at all that year, really, and the next time I did, he had stolen one of my vehicles we had left that needed to be fixed. It was the last straw for me, especially after we found a lot of our stuff stolen from out of our house that we had left behind and were planning to

213

use. We had words, and even though we called the cops, I didn't tell them where he was or when he was coming back to the property because we regained possession of our vehicle.

It would be a year later that we would see him again at a bar-b-que for Independence Day, once more out of jail but clean and sober from drugs. I was proud of him for getting off the drugs. It's not something that is easy to do. He moved to West Virginia, and I would occasionally see him when he came into town and was at Walmart. It wouldn't be until a year after that that we just so happened to go camping at the same time in the same place and ran into one another. He was still clean from heroin. And I was so proud of him for staying clean. He was his old self again, the same kid I grew up with who got into shenanigans together.

We were honestly partners in crime growing up. We would fake clean my room just to steal beer from my dad off the porch where he kept it. We would throw the bag back into my bedroom so it seemed like we were cleaning. We rode four-wheelers together and raced. One time, I nearly flipped it, and he helped me back into the house because I had pulled a muscle when I fell off the back of it, and then he put the four-wheeler up for me. My mom was out of town for her aunt's funeral, and my dad wasn't watching me. I was around twelve years old, maybe thirteen.

We once thought we found a dead body at a dumpster. So, the year is like 2009 and he and I were out in my car riding. Like I can't remember what we were doing or where we had gone, but we were in my purple Grand AM and coming down Power Dam Road in the dark when we passed by the dumpsters, and I caught a glimpse of something hanging out of them for just a second as my headlights passed over them. I asked him, "Was that a leg or foot? It looked like a leg dangling out the dumpster." He was like, "I'm pretty sure it was." So, I bust a U-turn at the stop sign and go back. I pull into the dumpster area and shine my headlights onto the dumpsters where sure enough, there was a leg dangling out of the dumpster. At some point, I was like, "We need to see if it's dead. Go poke it with a stick." Him: "I ain't poking it with a stick! You poke it with a stick!" Me: "You're the dude!" Him: "And?" Me: "Rock, paper, scissors?" Well, he lost. It was decided that it wasn't a dead body after I made my 16/17-year-old nephew poke it with a stick, and when he poked it with a stick, my headlights cut off, and he screamed my name, thinking I did it on purpose. We had made it back to the property and were in the middle of telling the story when my brother's ex-wife called, scared because she had found the "body" as well. He was like, "I got this." We rode back out, and he fucked with her for a few moments before telling her we already knew it wasn't a dead body.

It turned out the "body" was a scarecrow or an old Halloween prop. We told my dad what we had seen, and he made us go and make sure there wasn't a little kid or baby stuffed in there that had been murdered (there was not). I snapped a picture of him posing in front of the dumpster. He took the Timbaland boots it was wearing because they were in good condition for someone just to toss away. Out of everything we ever did together, when I think of him, this is the story I always think of.

Three weeks after running into him while camping and getting to spend some time together, I got the phone call from his mom out of her mind that he had overdosed. She dropped the phone mid-sentence, and the call was lost. I sat on my bed with my hands just in the air, trying to process what she had just said. He had overdosed? She called me back within a minute, and I asked her, "Is he dead?" It was undetermined at the moment. I was like, "he's been clean! How did he overdose? What was it?" She didn't know the details. So, I sat and waited for more updates. I messaged my other nephew, who was also raised as my little brother. He lived with my parents, and I helped put him off to school in the mornings.

I put a post up asking for prayers, and one of my aunts from my dad's side of the family was aware of what was happening, and we agreed to keep each other updated. I prayed. It's not something I do very often because every time I do, it seems my prayers go unanswered. But I had faith, and I prayed... and my expectation was what I knew it would be. My aunt messaged me he didn't make it. I lost it. My prayer had gone unanswered, and my faith wavered even more. They say tragedy and death happen outside of the hands of God, but God damn, does it make me angry when it happens. And that anger fuels my disbelief in a cycle of disbelief and faith. I waver. I falter. I fall. I rise. I believe. Rinse and repeat. It is so tiring... My husband had already lain down for bed because he had work the next day. I woke him up with my cries, and he was like, "What happened?" And I said the words out loud. "He overdosed. He's dead. He's gone." He tried to get me to calm down and lie down to go to sleep when my other nephew called me.

He began to explain on the phone in just bits and pieces of what had happened. He had gotten there, and my nephew was on the ground with blue lips and had already aspirated. They hit him twice with Narcan, but he didn't come back. He was on life support at the hospital, so family could come say goodbye. He had worked on him doing CPR for twenty minutes before the ambulance got there, but he couldn't save him. I told him it wasn't his fault.

It felt like an eternity waiting for his autopsy to be done and his body to be released for a funeral. On the day of his services, we drove to West Virginia and got a hotel and to the holler we went. I spent maybe ten minutes in the church before I had to go grab the bottle of 99 blackberries I had brought to leave in his casket. I had planned to drink it in his memory because the first time I got him drunk after turning twenty-one was with 99 blackberries. I drank on it all night because every time I walked into that church to see him, and I broke down. His sober buddy that was there told us a story we never thought we would hear. He had known my nephew had "the itch" again for heroin and was trying to do pills, cocaine, and meth to scratch the itch. I stood there, drunk, rage building in my chest at this supposed best friend for not telling anyone whenever he had the itch so we could watch him and keep him on track.

The next day was the funeral. It was tear-filled, and I was left empty and broken-hearted that my little brother was really gone. My little brother who danced around shouting, "I'm going to be an uncle!" when he found out I was pregnant. I wrapped his casket in a rebel flag because that was him. Rebel flags, rising four-wheelers, running the property, dirt bikes, mud bogging in his old Toyota, those are the memories I have of him. He even tried to teach me to drive an old granny stick shift in his dad's dually once. We tried to write raps together since we both loved Eminem. We did nearly everything together. I remember he used to stuff towels into my mom's bra and wear them while riding his big wheel on our front porch, donning sunglasses.

There was one time I went down to his house while he was in the garage, and he was like, "Come draw me some stuff on the walls." He had me draw pot leaves and mushrooms, all the while bragging to his friends that I was such a good artist and could draw anything. It took a session of therapy to realize that he truly supported me my whole life. He was my nephew, my little brother, and my first best friend. I was his "big sister," whom he envied like all little siblings do. My mother never directly praised me like he did. There was nothing I couldn't do in his eyes.

They played music as he was being put in the ground, and the one that tore me up and caught me off-guard was Number to Heaven by Justin Champagne. The words "we could drink a few beers in that old garage" did me in, and I broke down in heaving sobs. That was his playground, the garage. We drank in there. We partied in there. He helped us fix our car in that garage. The garage was him. And that song brought everything crashing down around me because he was gone and not coming back. It completely sank in he was dead as I had drifted the last week through disassociation from it all. I had gone through all the stages of grief and had landed in the last one of acceptance, and it hit me like a ton of bricks.

I have buried many people in my lifetime that I have loved. Friends, family, but him... he broke me. I would have hugged him if I knew it was going to be the last time I saw him. I would have said love you one more time before leaving. I would have waited longer to hear more of his stories because he always had a story to tell. I would have listened harder for one more laugh. I would have gone night fishing when he asked while we were camping. I would have stayed until I saw him off home. I would have messaged sooner instead of putting it off to hang out again. I would have had a beer instead of letting the crowd of people he had camping with him drown me out. I would give anything for just one more anything. But now he's gone, and there's a hole he left in his wake that can never be filled. And I am angry. I can't have just one more day with him. Drugs took him away when we all thought that day was gone and over with.

Now, my nightmares are filled with anxiety again. Anxiety from a time not so far away but also millions of miles in the past. Grief has a way of always reminding me of one of my deepest fears. Everyone I ever need always ends up leaving me alone. With every soul that is taken from me before their time should have been called, I feel like the bottom of the boat is going to fall out in my life and capsize me in deep waters where I will flounder and drown.

My nightmares keep that anxiety and fear alive like oxygen to a fire. It feels like I am walking around on hot coals made from glass, and each step cuts me deeper and deeper until I am crawling on my knees, and my heart is out on the floor, bleeding, torn, and barely beating. That's how deep my love goes, and my mind tortures me with it incessantly. I wish it would go away and melt into the past. But it won't. It will forever stay, and I will forever fall down and scrape my knees across those glass coals of hell.

Dear Diary,

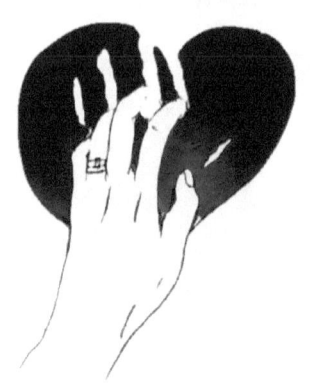

And like the little girl who had once reached out for affection and love and was struck down with apathy by people you are told live you most, you have shattered me like I was a child all over again. Why doesn't anybody ever love me...

Obligation definition:

- An act or course of action to which a person is morally or legally bound; a duty or commitment.
- The condition of being morally or legally bound to do something.
- A debt of gratitude for a service or favor.

Middle English (in the sense 'formal promise'): via Old French from Latin *obligatio(n-)*, from the verb *obligare*

I know I speak often about how my husband was my savior, but I don't think I talk about how much he is also a huge problem of my mental health issues. As much as he has built me up over the years, self-esteem-wise, he has also torn me down. Before and especially after I had my second child, he drank heavily and spent all his time partying down the hill with the renters. Another hot poker to my fragile soul and heart, he cheated on me, which in turn led to him stopping drinking altogether until he was working out of town and partying in his freedom. His talking to his ex is what drove my worth into the ground multiple times over the years, with the last time being the worst-case scenario.

I will never understand, know, or truly comprehend how he feels for me. One day, he says how much he loves me and the next, I'm his obligation. To him, he doesn't have a life. He has responsibility for the kids, and I'm his obligation that he will escape once the kids turn eighteen and are out of the house, no longer needing a double-parent household. I have always been an obligation. My mother's obligation was to just live long enough to where I would be old enough to make it on my own. There is no care behind the word, nor is there any love behind it. It's a word of duty that boils down to me being a burden. I'm a choice he didn't want, but he felt duty-bound to keep me because I had his kids.

All I have ever wanted in my life was for someone to love and care for me because they wanted to, not because they had to. That's what an obligation is. That's what I am. When my mom died, my sister told me she had to help me with this and that because she was my older sister. It was out of duty, out of obligation, that she helped me when she did because no one else was doing it and not because she wanted to help me out. Just another obligation to another person.

Whenever he tells me I am an obligation, I am reminded of not only every instance I have felt as one or a burden but also of the time when I read his messages to his ex. When he told her of how often he had thought of leaving and stayed because of the kids. Something else he has told me quite often. He says things like he wished he had listened to his mom and dad when they told him to leave me at the beginning of our relationship or when they told him not to marry me. He will say things like I trapped him with kids when he should have left when I miscarried the first time, but he was "too hooked on the pussy" to go, and I got pregnant again.

A pain rises in my chest whenever I hear it or remember it. Anxiety courses through me, and I feel my heart die a little each time. I swear, by the time I do die, there won't be anything left of it or the shadow of the little girl I feed crumbs of hopeless romanticism through the bars of the cell I now have her locked in. The remnants of Disney princesses gaining their prince and true love's kiss echo in my mind, telling me and her that love is real and not a façade created to give people a purpose to be together for more than procreation. Those Disney movies turned into adult romances and romcoms filled with hopeful aspirations of what love could be for me. But I fear that is all that exists for me is fictional romance and not the same unrequited love tales I have grown accustomed to reading and seeing.

There was a time when my husband would cook for me. It wasn't just solely my duty to fill that role all the time. He would cook breakfast. He would make dinner. But once he became the sole provider, his ego changed. He became dominating as if he were better than me, and I had expectations to meet that he had fallen short of and I had to make up when I was the one in the role of provider. But when I bring those things up, I am "bringing up the past" that doesn't matter in the present because I am the problem. I am the one failing as a parent and as a spouse just because I don't keep up with his expectations to the point where he says being depressed isn't an excuse because everyone is depressed, and they still do the shit they need to do.

It has become my duty as a wife to bend to his every want, every need, and every beck and call. I wash his clothes. I cook his food. I clean his house. I am a servant, a maid to him, just as I was to my parents and just like them, without him lifting a single finger to help outside of his role as a provider. I take care of him like a nurse when he is sick. I am the role of mother in his life, doing everything for him. I take care of his children, which undoubtedly is my single joy in life to be a mother myself, twenty-four hours a day, seven days a week, even when I myself was the one working to provide. I did all of that.

But even the joy I feel has its strains as I never have a moment's peace or moment's respite, and when I bring it up, he accuses me of never wanting my children, and I should have never spread my legs to have them if I want other people to watch them. I am the only one that cooks for them. I put them off to school. I deal with school when they call. I help them with homework. I read to them. I take care of them when they are sick. I take them to the doctor's office. I do everything for my kids and mostly do it alone. I have my kids by myself for the majority of the time, and even when he is home, I am still the one dealing with them arguing and fighting. I am the one disciplining them. I am the one trying to teach them to do chores and be responsible.

But I am then cast as a bad mother for just simply wanting time to myself or a day to just us as few as those days come. Date nights, vacations, a honeymoon, none of those things are luxuries for me as they have been for everyone else I have known. It's taxing on me to be the only one to do any and everything for everyone in the household, but if I mention any of it, I am the bad guy. I am the imperfect wife and the imperfect mother of evil intent, and I am put on trial for it all. I have no personal support system. I have no one in my corner to validate what I feel and experience. So, I bear these feelings in silence and contempt because speaking out loud is a crime.

It is a crime to want and need my own identity outside of the roles I have been assigned in this relationship. My identity is wife, mother, and maid, and those roles come with obligations that have to be fulfilled or threats are made. As a wife, I have to bend to his every need and exploit myself sexually just to have his attention, or he says he will find someone else who will. If I can't mother his children to his expectations or clean his house, he can find someone who will. All I want is to be loved and needed as such, but instead I must comply if I don't want to be alone. I fear loneliness because it's all I have ever known. Those Disney movies I coveted so much as a child set my expectations for love too high, and now, I drown and flounder in those hopes and aspirations. He uses the fears I have of abandonment against me knowingly and exploits them for his own selfish gains.

He was once my knight in shining armor, saving me from the tower I had been locked away in, guarded by fairytale dragons of fire and damnation. But now, he has imprisoned me in a new tower where Dr. Jekyll and Mr. Hyde take turns ravaging my psyche with words of love and then words of malice, moments in which I would have preferred the dragon-guarded tower instead of a false sense of security. And I never know which is the true version I am tethered to, for there are days they are both present with acts of love then words of disdain. The words of venom he spews break me and shatter me and I make so many excuses for him as I did my parents as an adolescent.

I never wanted to be another obligation. I never wanted to feel again as if I were a duty or a burden that had to be taken care of instead of wanted. In every relationship I have ever had, I have never been wanted. I have always been a filler for whatever void or purpose they needed to fulfill. Every time I think it is time to bring my walls down because I am safe, I am reminded I am not safe from pain or heat break or torment because I am not what is needed or wanted but something that "will do" as a "second or only choice" because their first choice fell through going up in smoke and flames. I am who they settle for and not what they truly covet. I am an obligation, as simple as said. I am not loved because a person wouldn't say that to someone they loved or treat them in such ways that they feel as if they don't belong or shouldn't even exist.

Love is not full of hateful words and malevolence spouting regret. I am a regret in wishes to go back in time to undo the mistake made. To unring a bell that had been rung because I am a failure at everything they aspire me to be. I am flawed and broken. I am cracked and leak out everything they wish I were. I am unwanted and only around because it is the right thing to do for the children and not because he cannot live without me. I am the sex toy for when he needs sexual release but not companionship and intimacy. I am everything he wishes I wasn't. I am me and even I hate me, but I had thought he saw a glimmer that I am reminded of that I should have. But I do not glimmer or shine. I am a blown lightbulb, and he stumbles through the dark of my essence. I am a black hole, the embodiment of the abyss, and he will never love me. Not like I want, not like I need, if not ever. He has always loved someone else, and I will never be her. I walk in her shadow, and I hate myself for believing and thinking in the hope that he did. I begged for his love and attention as he dwindled the day, liking and ogling other women on social media, shaking their asses and tits. My begging is answered with futility. I will never be of importance to him. I will always be the ball and chain of duty, responsibility, and obligation, nothing more and nothing less.

He told her Lips of an Angel by Hinder was his song to her, and I will never forget the line "sometimes I wish she was you." I wish he were happy I was just me and not wanting me to be someone else he loved or still loves. I will never be good enough or worthy enough in his eyes, no matter how perfect of a wife I try to be, and he will always love her more than what he feels for me because, as he said, he's here for the kids and nothing more.

These anxieties triggered a nightmare about ghosts from the past. In the nightmare, he openly told me about his affair and how he wanted it to be a polyamorous thing, which I vehemently said no to over and over again. He was cheating with the woman who had caused our issues. After several times in the dream of handing him my wedding rings and they magically reappeared on my hand, I gave them to him one final time. It was then that he said so you're just giving up on me and our family. I told him no, that I was taking the kids and leaving. I wasn't doing what he wanted to do with the relationship. I jumped out of the vehicle we were in, and the dream ended. I had anxiety for days after that nightmare, palpitating anxiety. That nightmare stuck in my head and caused paranoia to consume me. It took about two weeks and a couple of therapy sessions for me to realize it was all in my head and not happening in real life.

No one will ever love me like I deserve to be loved as proven throughout my history with men or family. Everyone bases my worth on what I can do for them as opposed to who I am. People wonder why I am depressed and suicidal and can't ever function normally. This is why. No one ever wants me. They all always look at me as a burden or an obligation, a fuck up that just ruins their life. And I am so tired of feeling rejected and unwanted. I will never be good enough for anyone because I am me, and I can't change who I am as a person.

No one will consume themselves in me like I consume myself in loving them. I often wonder how much he thinks of her and how many times he wishes he was with her and not me. I bet it's often because I am nothing, nothing but a waste of space simply here to just to be a doormat and a warm body to lie beside at night so his loneliness and yearning for her doesn't consume him and to quieten the demons he quells beneath his murky surface. I am a space holder who one day will be removed and filled with what he truly desires. Someone who isn't me.

Dear Diary,

Recalling abuse never happens in chronological order. Recalling abuse doesn't start at the beginning and doesn't move through each year, recounting what happened in every single instance. Recalling abuse is sporadic and an untamed thought pattern. When I was in therapy for what short amount of time I spent there, when it got to the point where we were supposed to start talking about my abuse, the therapist asked me to start at the beginning. I couldn't. I didn't know how. I wracked my brain sitting there, trying to remember my first instance of abuse, but I couldn't form any words. Was I four? Was I three? Was I nine? I couldn't remember.

However, when I think of something that happened to me when I was a teenager, a floodgate will open, and every instance of abuse cycles through my mind as if it all happened at once. It's called post-traumatic stress disorder and trauma for a reason. Our brain builds walls around it. Our brain tries to separate it from our core memories because of the amount of fear and pain we suffered at the moment in question. Our brain doesn't want that experience to become a part of who we are and how we are shaped without realizing that by separating it out causes more of a traumatic experience than allowing it to remain with our normal memories.

I tend to feel like this happens mostly with a trauma bond; at least, it was in my experience. My abuse came from the people that were supposed to love me and protect me. They were supposed to create happy moments for me to remember. Instead, I have nights where I wake from a dead sleep with my stomach hurting and a panic attack shaking me to my core. I don't remember what happened to me in my sleep. I don't know if I was woken up by my mom in a rage or what it was, but I awake to PTSD panic, and it's the most frightening experience I have ever lived through.

I can go to bed completely normal. I could have a normal day, a normal week, or even a normal month. But around the twilight hours of sleep, I would begin to toss and turn, with my stomach hurting. I would feel nauseous. I would feel like I needed to vomit, and in some cases, I did vomit. Sometimes, vomiting would ease my stomach trouble, and I would just have a mild panic attack. No breathing issues. Just a little hot and itchy. A majority of the time, those easy panic attacks were not the case. I would vomit. I would shit. I would gasp for air. At times, it was so bad I had to go to the ER for epinephrine to breathe. It felt like my throat was closing. It felt exactly like how having a severe food allergy would feel. My heart would pound in my chest, up into my throat, into my ears. An electrical feeling would shoot up my back, starting at the base of my spine, and wrap and intertwine itself through every disc. It felt like someone was reaching into my back and using my spine as the control rod of a puppet, and I was the puppet on stage, splayed out for all to see what a horrible mess I was.

Sometimes, I would black out from the lack of oxygen. I have rolled around on the ground, trying to breathe. I have urinated on myself because I thought I was really dying. I have crawled into the bottom of a bathtub, turned the shower on to cold, and sat in the water trying to cool my body down. I have sat on the toilet, unable to move from body fatigue as my body pumps every ounce of adrenaline to my heart to keep me from shutting down. I have never really timed my experiences, but usually, it's around twenty or thirty minutes from start to finish when I am able to move again without feeling like I am using every ounce of will to live. However, at the moment, it feels like an eternity. It feels like what they describe hell to be or for a near-death experience. It feels like it will never end.

I have said before that it doesn't always happen when I am asleep. When I have sensory overload, if I don't calm myself down, I go into panic mode. I try to extradite myself from the situation at hand, causing sensory overload, but sometimes, it's stacked moments from the day. Sometimes, it's the grating voice of my children asking me questions over and over while I have asked them for just a moment to myself. At times, it has been my own cause. Working myself up over stupid things. And then there are times when I can't identify the trigger at all. It's hard to fix a trigger when the trigger is unknown.

I don't sit around every single day and replay what happened to me throughout my life over and over in my head. I bury most of it. I can watch movies and shows and not be triggered by events occurring in them that happened to me. On occasion, I will find something that gets my heart racing and me chewing my nails, but it hasn't caused me to have a panic attack as described above. It's only caused anxiety. I buried the emotional trauma of my childhood and teenage years, and I strive every day to live as normal of a life as I possibly can.

My trauma bond made me believe that my life was normal, like every other kid's life. I didn't know that other kids weren't spanked with a wooden paddle. I didn't know other kids weren't struck in the face for punishment. I didn't know other kids weren't belittled for their appearance or for peculiar behavior, such as wetting the bed. I thought my experiences, although emotionally and mentally harrowing, were completely normal experiences. It wasn't until later, when I was older that I realized that it all was abuse. And by the time I realized it was abuse, I knew that there was nothing I could do about it.

Sure, I could have told an adult at school or a counselor what happened at home, but when my sister did that, nothing happened. Her only escape was to move out. She had a license. She had a job. I wasn't allowed those things. My father told me he wouldn't allow me the chance to leave like he had my sister. But of course, they wouldn't. At that point, I took care of the household. I cooked. I cleaned. I took care of my mother, whose health was declining. I had been self-sufficient since I was about eleven years old. I could have made it on my own had I tried and emancipated myself the same way my sister had. But a part of me didn't want to reveal my parents' abuse. I didn't want my mother or father to go to jail for what they had done to me or to my sister. My trauma bond made me feel empathy because even though there were bad times, there were also good times. I felt as if the good times made up enough for the bad ones that it wasn't as serious as it was.

I always imagined my sister would save me. My sister had dealt with her fair share of abuse while living in the house. She was beaten far worse than I was. She was more than sympathetic to how I lived. She was empathetic. She knew what it was like. But she was also apathetic. She felt as if I didn't receive enough punishment. So, one day, she logged into my Yahoo account at her house and printed off messages between me and a boy I had been talking to. He was my "online boyfriend." But I didn't want to talk to him anymore, so I was trying to end things, and he wouldn't take the answer I was giving him. I cussed at him, telling him to leave me the fuck alone. I used fuck a lot in the messages to try and get my point across. She mailed it to my mother anonymously and even arrived at the house to witness what was going to happen. She stood there and let my mother beat me for swearing at a boy that made me uncomfortable to talk to. She says I was sitting in the chair when Mom slapped me across the face. I may have started in the chair because that part is fuzzy. I may have tried to run from my spot in the chair, and she chased me to where I had been standing, but what I do remember is the final place where she hit me repeatedly. I was back against a beam where a wall used to stand that they removed to make the living room bigger. She watched her beat my face as I covered my head with my hands to appease the blows. Whether she knew she had ripped my earrings out, I don't know, but my mom did. And the only concern she showed was when my mother tried to pick up the computer to throw it outside because it was a heavy computer, and my mother might hurt herself.

Later, she would tell me that she didn't think mom would lose it the way she did, and she had to make sure her kids that were there didn't get hurt in mom's rage. I can understand that. But she could have stopped her. Instead, she allowed something to happen that was her own fault because she wanted to prove that I wasn't as perfect as my mother thought I was. She now just says it was one smack to the face, and that was it. I don't know if it's her own trauma response and needs to glorify our mother and make it seem like I wasn't abused because she was beaten more than I was, but she denies my testimony of how it happened. I do remember my sister-in-law walking up on the porch while she was trying to throw the computer out the door. Between then and when my mother apologized for losing control on me and looked my ear over when she noticed the blood dried on it, I can't remember anything. All I remember is her rage and trying to shelter my face.

I never really forgave my sister for that moment. But today, I do, and I release her from her own accountability for what happened, whether she feels guilty or not. Where I see someone that could have stopped my mother, there was a person standing there reliving her own abuse at my mother's hands, trying to ignore it. What I thought was apathy was fear.

Whenever I think about this one time my mother beat me, it brings up memories in flashes of every other time in my life when my mother had struck me or whipped me or verbally assaulted me or mentally abused me. It doesn't happen in chronological order because all those memories are stored in the same place in my brain, and when I open that box, they all pop out at once.

Dear Diary,

I still have nightmares about the people who bullied me in school. They held control over me throughout the years. If I had a crush on any of the people in the clique they ran in, I was humiliated for it. The only solace I get from those nightmares is when I awaken and I roll over to find my husband sound asleep beside me. He chose me. He loved me for me. He married me. I am his best friend, and he is mine. I was his princess that he saved from the tower that her parents kept her prisoner in fashioned out of a double wide. I was Cinderella. I was Rapunzel. I was a princess at the very bare fact of what Grimm Brothers' princesses experienced in their twisted tales. I wasn't allowed to watch Rated R movies with sex scenes and had to turn my head at 20 years old. Some of my best friends were 16-year-olds, and they were a "bad influence" on *me*.

My husband saved me. He found me locked away and in need, in trouble. Drowning, he pulled me to safety. He set me free. And that is why I will always love him. My prince came for me. My prince let me finish becoming an adult. He might not have been in shining armor, but he was a savior nonetheless and saved me from that tall tower with a lock and key. And now, I am a queen, his queen. He showers me with the love and acceptance I wanted while growing up. He doesn't shame my weight but instead insists I eat. He was the guy my mother told me would never love me.

When I first met him, he was such a gorgeous, sexy specimen. I honestly couldn't believe someone as attractive as him was interested in me. He never pressured me for sex nor used me for sex. He didn't touch me without permission or invitation. I figured he was one of the rare guys that liked big, beautiful women, but no. I wasn't his type at all, but he still found me beautiful. He calls me Buttercup, and I like to think it's because my soul shines so brightly, like the sun shining down on a flower. He has always told me he loved my soul. I used to equate that to a guy saying you're not the prettiest thing to look at, but you have a great personality. I couldn't figure out how he would be attracted to me if he didn't find me pretty. But my anxieties have always done the talking in my mind.

While watching a movie, he made a comment about how he wished he knew how attractive people fall in love with unattractive people. I was like, "Um?" and pointed between the two of us. He asked me, "What did you mean by that," thinking I was saying he was ugly. I told him, "Because I am ugly." The blinking, incredulous stare he gave me after I said that told me all I ever needed to hear without him telling me all the time. He thought I was beautiful and didn't understand why I said I wasn't and thought I wasn't. He didn't need to reassure me at that moment by telling me I was beautiful because his face said it all.

In that moment, the little girl inside of me squealed in delight. The person who was supposed to love me and supposed to think I was beautiful did indeed believe I was beautiful and loved me for me. All the many times that I have tried to diet, my husband has never reminded me that I was on a diet (Other than when I was diagnosed with diabetes, and he helped me curb my appetite for sweet food). He has never pressured me to lose weight, even when I ballooned up to cow proportions and felt like a fat blob of unnecessary space. He still found me attractive. And even as I struggle currently with my weight, he doesn't say anything about it. He doesn't tell me I NEED to lose weight. But when I am going too far with dieting, he does say something. He tells me to eat. He tells me the diet is too harsh and to eat. He reminds me that my being healthy eating is better than my being unhealthy by not eating. He reminds me that I have daughters that I need to set a precedent for and teach them that my unhealthy eating disorders are not something that should even exist for girls. That no matter how big or small you are, you are beautiful just as you are.

Dear Diary,

There were snickers here, and there were snickers there while I was in my formidable years of elementary school, but middle school through high school were the ones that crushed my soul the most. I had hoped that boys would like me in middle school. I was always viewed as one of the guys, and there was a crossroads as I stepped over the threshold into middle school. I was still viewed as one of the guys. I had guy friends. But I was also seen as ugly and fat, and boys didn't like me as a girl.

Well, at least one boy did. We rode the bus together to and from school and spent every single day talking or listening to my portable CD player. In eighth grade, I asked him to be my "boyfriend," and even though he said yes, we weren't really boyfriend and girlfriend. It was just titles, but that title was so important to me. If you flash forward just a bit, there was a moment in one of my classes when we were in the library, and one of the boys who helped harass me with others came up to me and asked me if I would "go out" with another boy in the class. Mind you, this boy I had caught snickering and pointing and making fun of me along with the guy asking for him.

"No," I said.

"Why?" he asked.

And I said something that was mean. I was mean for just a moment to serve my justice to him.

"Because it's John!" I replied.

And bless her soul, my best friend didn't skip a beat and added, "Plus, she's dating Ray."

I didn't find boys attractive that were mean to me. I would find some sort of flaw and focus on it to keep from being hurt. John had a lazy eye. I focused on it. I used it as my excuse to say no. But John had been ugly to me without any type of imperfections. He was ugly through his actions toward me. And he heard me say what I said and over the summer, he had the biggest glow up. And I was happy for him for that even though I never told him. He not only changed on the outside by losing weight and showing his personality through the clothes he chose to wear, but he changed on the inside as well. That glow-up is what made him the most attractive person to me on campus.

Now, I never did date him. I am certain I lost that opportunity the previous year, and I never tried to investigate it because he deserved to have someone who didn't think the mean things I had thought about him with his appearance. But as I said, ugly was on the inside and out to me. I think what is lost on a lot of younger people is they solely focus just on the outside appearance because they have been indoctrinated into it. Magazines, TV, music videos, and fashion all of those say if you aren't this way, then you need to be, or no one will like you.

But eighth grade... eighth grade became the one year of mortification that altered me forever. One of the reasons I said no to John was because of what had already happened with me and that group of boys that always tormented me. It shaped my view of myself. It anchored my body dysmorphia. It solidified every single negative thought I had ever thought of myself because of people who spat them at me. There was a new boy that year in the group of boys. Each year, we were put on four teams, and in eighth grade, those four were combined into two. So, a new guy had come along, and he was cute. But they were horrible boys.

They had him pretend like he wanted to be my boyfriend. So, at lunch, he walked over to my table while I sat with my friends eating and asked me to be his girlfriend. I was a bit taken aback but smiled, but that smile faded when I looked behind to see all the boys laughing.

"She fell for it!"

And then he started laughing. He was the last straw that broke my spirit. That's when I stopped eating. I didn't eat breakfast. I didn't eat lunch. I associated that moment with food. Food was the reason boys didn't like me. Food made me fat no matter how little I ate. And I heard it from everyone. So, I stopped eating. I stopped eating in public, period. I would only eat at home. I couldn't be embarrassed about eating at home because there weren't mean people there to point out my flaws and make me feel even more horrible about how I looked. Except there was. My mother.

My mother made sure to drive the nail in the coffin when it came to my body dysmorphia. "You shouldn't eat that, or you will gain weight." "Haven't you had enough to eat?" "I already made you something to eat. Don't eat that. It's your dad's." The only thing I was eating at that point was a snack when I got home from school and dinner. I became a binge eater. I would even eat food I didn't even like during the binges. I would feel guilty about eating, and then dread would set in. "Oh no! I'm going to gain weight from eating all of that." So, I did what every other binger would do. If I ate too much, especially if it made me nauseous after, I would vomit it back up. My mother displaced her own body dysmorphia on me. My mother chased the trend diets, the diet pills, and anything she could find to get her body back she used to have. When she would buy new diet pills, she bought them for me, too.

I don't know if I will ever be whole and not broken into millions of little pieces. I don't know if I will ever heal from the abuse I was subjected to throughout my life. I don't know if I will ever be able to look in the mirror and truly accept the way I look. I like to think that one day I will be able to do these things and I believe that it will come from within rather than staking my salvation from those around me on the outside. I have spent my entire life wondering why I wasn't loved as I was, why I wasn't like the other kids. Why did I have a mountain that I had to constantly climb to obtain love from anyone at all. Neglect has made me the damaged vessel that I am today.

I'm not sure if I will ever acknowledge that self-love was my road to recovery. Did I truly love myself? Others profess that it's the only way to obtain the affection of those around because who would love someone who doesn't even love themselves? Even as the words leave my lips that I don't love myself, I *know* that it's a lie screaming from within me because if I didn't love myself at all, I wouldn't search out those to love the broken pieces. I wouldn't care about anything at all. I wouldn't care about what others thought of me. I would be narcissistic and apathetic with all aspects of life, and I know that I love with every fiber of my being every person in my life that is important to me. I love them with a deadly passion, a lethal grasp that I stake my life over their life at any given moment if they need me to do so. I would walk to hell and back to keep them safe and loved.

My children have taught me that they are my mirror and reflect back what I can't see in myself. Where I see poor parenting due to my mental health, they see love and tell me. Where I see self-loathing, they admire me. When I get past these layers, I feel their love and see their truths about me. I am worth love. I am enough.

Our job as parents is to teach them love, compassion, and empathy. It is our job to protect them from the burdens that wrap around their shoulders like a deadened weight. It is our job to let them know that they can come to us with whatever troubles their heart and tell us what is on their mind. We aren't here to make their lives difficult or to make sure they have a "thick skin" to survive the cruelty of the world. We are here to let them know that no matter how hard the world makes our lives, whenever they walk into our arms, it is pure and unconditional love that they feel within themselves instead of disgust or judgment. We owe it to our children that shaped and molded us adults to help them when they are in need just as they have helped us whenever we are in need. It may have been an "I love you" when you needed to hear it most or a hug so deep that you could feel their heartbeat as yours when you needed to feel love. It is your job and responsibility as their parent to let them know at every stage in their life that they are still your child even when their hair grays and wrinkles splotch their face. Until we die and even in the great beyond after death, it is our job to wrap them in love so they never feel like they are utterly alone in this world of apathy and hatred.

I still shrink in space when someone approaches me too quickly, and I still flinch away if someone raises their hand around me in fear I will be hit. If someone raises their voice around me, my instinct is to get up and clean even when everything is already clean. Loud voices cause me to have panic attacks. I constantly think when I enter a room that they were all talking about me and quickly stopped. I believe people stare at me and think ugly thoughts about how I look. I overthink and overanalyze every single little thing to the point I have imaginary arguments in my head with people. There are conversations and arguments in my head with people I haven't even spoken to in years that I wish I could go back and say something else as opposed to what I had tried to say. I can't talk because I have no voice of advocacy for myself. So, I sit and drown, locked away inside of my own mind.

If I could travel back in time, I would travel back for just one thing. It's not to relive a moment. It's not to fancy any particular time that I was happy. It would be to see that little girl staring at herself in the mirror, wondering why boys didn't like her, wondering why her mother said awful things to her about her weight, wondering why her mother treated her the way she did, wondering why she was made to be different, wondering why she was ever born at all, and I would hug her and tell her three things:

1) You are beautiful.
2) You are perfect.

And lastly

3) I love you.

Dear Diary,

I set that little girl I had locked away free... and I feel...

at peace.

Darkest Dream

I'm running far away
To escape this place
I look to the stars for the face
Who will save me and take me away
His hands brush away the tears
My body shudders with his touch
Within him I see so clear
His image slowly fades to black
He's the one
That we dream of
The one who can save us all
I keep trying
To find the one man
Who will save us from the darkness
All one thousand
Kids mistreated
Who feel lonely
Need to be saved from this horrible Place
Flown Away
Steered away from
A suicide life
A suicide life
I'm running from the field of tears
And falling into a world of fears
I reach for his outstretched hand
I can't reach him
I can't touch him

I'm falling into
The darkest dream
Where all innocence is lost
Everything is lost
The lightning strikes
I hold his hand tight
Hanging from the Cliffside so high
My eyes are pleading with his
Save me
Help me
I keep trying
To find the one man
Who will save us from the darkness
All one thousand
Kids mistreated
Who feel lonely
Need to be saved from this horrible Place
Flown Away
Steered away from
A suicide life
A suicide life
I'm running from the field of tears
And falling into a world of fears
I reach for his outstretched hand
I can't reach him
I can't touch him
I'm falling into
The darkest dream
Where all innocence is lost
Everything is lost
Let me live
As I fall through the air

I can only remember
He was never there
They're jumping one by one
Into a sea of fiery hell
He flies in
But he's too late
His hopes have sank
There's no one left to save
All their lives
They hoped and prayed
That he would come
On the darkest day
But now they're gone
He is useless
No one gives a damn
They're mean and cruel
I keep trying
To find the one man
Who will save us from
The darkness
All one thousand
Kids mistreated
Who feel lonely
Need to be saved from this
Horrible Place
Flown Away
Steered away from
A suicide life
A suicide life
I'm running from the field of tears
And falling into a world of fears

I reach for his outstretched hand
I can't reach him
I can't touch him
I'm falling into
The darkest dream
Where all innocence is lost
Everything is lost

Belong

I can't
Believe
Exactly why I feel this way
It feels
So wrong
And I really need to find a way
To somehow get rid of it
Cause with you people
I can't
Belong
Somehow
Someway
I will find a way
To be so
Perfect
For you
I want to match you
In everything you do
I'll be the best
That I possibly can
Cause with you people
I can't
Belong
I'm so different
Than everybody else
I envy them and the looks they get
Why can't I be,
Perfect like them?
So I can

Belong
Some
Tell me
That people like that
Have nothing going for them
But see
Whenever they smile they break
The hearts of the people around
Because they're beautiful and perfect
Unlike me
Why can't I be seen,
For exactly who I am?
I don't want to be
Perfect like them
Because one day I'll be me
That's more perfect than life itself
Because just me
Myself
I will belong
I won't need to hide anymore
I will
Belong

We Died Right There

Tears stream from my misty eyes
Why, why did you have to die?
Your life
I know
Was full of pain
The scars on your wrists never did fade
Your father was always gone
When he was around
He said you were stupid and wrong
Your mother always had to yell
Each day your face turned more and more pale
They pushed you past the edge again
You were falling to your death
When I tried to catch you
Your blood ran cold and went everywhere
And you, died right there
The tears on your blood stained face
It always hid your emotions from being traced
Your eyes hid all the blame and crying
Hanging in the fire was all your lies
Me and you
We were always one of a kind
Over and over
We were born into this life
Now my hand remains without yours to hold
So
I know
The rain will always pour and storm
They laid you slowly in your grave

I kissed my rose and tossed it in with the rain
I'll no longer have you to talk to
So now I know
I will fall with you
Because
They
They pushed you past the edge again
You were falling to your death when I jumped in
Your blood ran cold with mine and went everywhere
And we
We died right there

Daddy

Daddy
Please don't yell
Cause you're making mommy cry
I know that you are angry
But it's not her fault its mine

Daddy
Please don't scream
I promise I'll be good
I know I'm not perfect
And I know you think that I should be

Daddy
Don't be mad
I promise that I'll try
But you've gotta stop yelling
Because I hate seeing mommy cry

Daddy
We can't be angels
We don't have wings to fly
We have no halos
But I'll be the best this time

Daddy
I love you
Please don't make mommy cry

Others Don't

A boy sat in an old hotel room
With a gun to his head
With his finger on the trigger
He started to wonder
Exactly what went wrong?
This is what happens when no one'll listen
When no one'll lend a helping hand
People forgive and people forget
But others don't
A girl sat on her bed
With the sharpest blade she's ever seen
She looked in her mirror
And saw the girl
She'll never be
A kid
Stood on the edge of a bridge
He looked down at the gray waters
He turned his head and saw his best friend
He got down that day
He lived to tell
You'll never know
If you'll see him again
This is what happened when someone listens
When someone lends a helping hand
This kid learned to forgive and forget
But others don't
It comes from the heart
To forgive and forget

Broken Home

Why do you look at me,
When all you do is see through me?
Don't judge me
Don't act like you know me
Don't smile and act so great
You don't know night from day
My life is all okay
Although I live a broken life
In a broken home
The way I dress scares everyone
I'm different
I'm not a flower
Why don't you let me be me?
And let me be something
Out of this broken life
And broken home
You see me with the bruises
You asked me all the same questions
Is your father drugging you?
Is your mother beating you?
Why can't you just leave me the hell alone?
I'm not that different from you or you
I just want to be known for me not you
All you are is a freaking drug head they say
Deeps inside your fears are all there
Your life is not alright
Cause you live in a broken home

I Run

The scars on my wrist will eventually fade
But the hurt and frustration will always remain
It feels like I've been thrown into a bottomless pit
The ground will never come, it I'll never hit
My love is like a scar it will eventually fade
But the pain that I went through will always stay the
same
You cut me like a knife and now all I do is cry
I try to forget your smile but all you do
Is give me pain to overcome
This game will never be won
Who would call this game fun?
Cause from you I run
I tell people I'm over it
That I'm done I'm through
But even those people say that I'm still obsessed with
you
Obsession is a big word too long for your brain
You're just a dumb boy but my life from me you
drain
So I run

I'll Be Gone

Every day we go through this every day
You hate my style
I wish I could get away from this place
From my faded dream
Away from the same old face
So I can be what I want to be
I'll be gone and you will never find me
You'll hear my song and wonder why you could not
see me for me
This is me you only get what you see
I'll be gone and you'll be left with my song
When I'm gone you'll see how happy I couldn't be
Because of you
You wouldn't let me express my individuality
One morning you'll wake up and you'll see
My room is bare and my bed empty
I won't miss this same damn place
I won't look back for your face
You won't see me again
No you won't
I'll be gone

NOTE FROM THE AUTHOR

Mental illness presents in many different ways. Delusions, hallucinations, mood changes, behavior changes, and many other things are symptoms of the chemical imbalance not being appropriately treated. If you or a loved one suffers from mental illness, please do not hesitate to get them help when they seem to have gone off their medication or are having a more challenging time coping with their ailments. They may need a medication change or a new evaluation to ensure they weren't misdiagnosed with one illness over another.

Those who suffer from mental illness, please, never hesitate to reach out when you feel your reality isn't your own. If you feel like you are having a psychotic episode, please reach out for help. There are many people that are eager and willing to help you get to a state of mind that is not abusive to your psyche.

If you are in a crisis, please call your doctor or 911.

If you don't feel comfortable talking to the doctor, reach out to one of the following crisis hotlines:

Text HOME or E.M.M. to 741741 to speak to someone about anxiety, depression, suicide, or any other mental instability

Call 1-800-273-8255 to speak to someone on the National Suicide hotline

Call 1-800-931-2237 to speak to someone on the National Crisis Hotline

Call 1-877-870-4673 to speak to someone on the Samaritan's HelpLine if you just need someone to talk to

Call 1-800-950-6264 to speak to someone on the NAMI Crisis Helpline or email info@nami.org

Call 1-800-395-5755 to speak to someone to share in your Grief/Loss

Call 1-800-DONT-CUT to speak to someone on the S.A.F.E. (Self Abuse Finally Ends) Helpline

Below are more helplines for crisis help:

Crisis #s (Teens Under 18)

Girls and Boys Town 1-800-448-3000

Hearing Impaired 1-800-448-1833

Youth Crisis Hotline 1-800-448-4663

Teen Hope Line 1-800-394-HOPE

Crisis #s (Any Age)

United Way Crisis Helpline 1-800-233-HELP

Christian Oriented Hotline 1-877-949-HELP

Social Security Administration 1-800-772-1213

Suicide

Suicide Hotline 1-800-SUICIDE (784-2433)

Suicide Prevention Hotline 1-800-827-7571

Deaf Hotline 1-800-799-4TTY

Holy Spirit Teenline (717) 763-2345 or 1-800-722-5385

Crisis Intervention (Harrisburg) (717) 232-7511 or 1- 888-596-4447

Carlisle Helpline (717) 249-6226

Crisis Intervention (York) (717) 851-5320 or 1-800-673-2496

Please, do not hesitate to reach out. Your life matters!

Author Bio

Kasey Thompson, formally known as Kasey Hill, has lived in Franklin County, VA for most of her adult life. Spending two years in journalism in high school, and a few articles published in the Franklin News Post, she built much of her young adult life around reading and writing. Starting her penmanship in 2008, she has spread her wings into the fiction side of writing. She has various book series published, various poetry books, and many short stories circulating for anthologies as she pushes her passions forth into the writing community. Her debut novel *Surviving Sarah* was the catalyst for her drive to promote mental health awareness through fiction. As a person that suffers mental health issues herself, she finds it cathartic to write about it and help spread awareness to people that they are not alone as well as destigmatize mental health in society. You can find her books online.